The Lilac Tunnel

My Journey with Samantha

by Erin Falligant

American Girl®

Published by American Girl Publishing

17 18 19 20 21 22 23 QP 10 9 8 7 6 5 4 3 2 1

Cover image by Michael Dwornik and Juliana Kolesova

Library of Congress Cataloging-in-Publication Data
Falligant, Erin.
The lilac tunnel : my journey with Samantha / Erin Falligant.
pages cm. — (BeForever)
Summary: "What if you, as a girl trying to adjust to her new stepfamily, suddenly found yourself in Samantha's world at the start of the 20th century? Join Samantha on exciting adventures. Your journey back in time can take whatever twists and turns you choose, as you select from a variety of options in this multiple-ending story."— Provided by publisher.
ISBN 978-1-60958-416-0 (paperback) — ISBN 978-1-60958-492-4 (ebook)
1. Plot-your-own stories. [1. Time travel—Ficton. 2. Stepfamilies—Fiction. 3. Plot-your-own stories.] I. Title.
PZ7.F1959Li 2014 [Fic]—dc23 2014015499

For Nicki, Holly, Alex, and Kenley,
whose imaginations take
us on great journeys

BeForever™

The adventurous characters you'll meet in
the BeForever books will spark your curiosity
about the past, inspire you to find your voice
in the present, and excite you about your future.
You'll make friends with these girls as you share
their fun and their challenges. Like you, they are
bright and brave, imaginative and energetic,
creative and kind. Just as you are, they are
discovering what really matters: Helping others.
Being a true friend. Protecting the earth.
Standing up for what's right. Read their stories,
explore their worlds, join their adventures.
Your friendship with them will BeForever.

A Journey Begins

This book is about Samantha, but it's also about a girl like you who travels back in time to Samantha's world of 1904. You, the reader, get to decide what happens in the story. The choices you make will lead to different journeys and new discoveries.

When you reach a page in this book that asks you to make a decision, choose carefully. The decisions you make will lead to different endings. (Hint: Use a pencil to check off your choices. That way, you'll never read the same story twice.)

Want to try another ending? Read the book again—and then again. Find out what happens to you and Samantha when you make different choices.

Before your journey ends, take a peek into the past, on page 186, to discover more about Samantha's time.

1

There's a knock on the bedroom door. I figure it's my new stepsister, Gracie, who's been coming in and out all morning. It's her room, too, so I *have* to let her in. With a sigh, I roll off the bed and open the door. I'm surprised to see not Gracie, but my stepmom.

She glances at the suitcase on the bed behind me. "Need help unpacking?"

I shake my head. I'm spending the summer here in Plattsburgh, New York, with my dad, his new wife, and her daughter, Gracie. I've been here for only a day and a half, but I'm already counting down the days till I can go back to my mom's house in New York City. It's funny—I just moved into a house full of people, but somehow I still feel as if I'm all on my own.

I miss my best friend and neighbor, Stella. I miss my own room and my cat, Maggie. I miss pulling out my laptop and my cell phone whenever I want because Dad says I can use them for only an hour a day. Most of all, I miss my mom. She thought I should spend some time with my dad to get to know his new family, but I miss my *old* family—the way things were a couple of years ago when my mom and dad were still together. Why can't things just go back to the way they were?

2

My stepmom comes into the room and sees the jewelry I've laid out on the dresser. She "oohs" and "aahs" over a friendship bracelet that Stella made for me before I left home. I can tell that my stepmom is trying to be nice, but I'm just not in the mood for conversation.

"I have something that I think you might like," she says, her eyes hopeful. "I'll be right back."

As my stepmom leaves the room, five-year-old Gracie pokes her face through the doorway. "What're you doing?" she asks.

"Nothing," I mumble. Gracie has been glued to me ever since I got here. It's hard enough to share a room—complete with twin beds and pink princess bedspreads—but Gracie wants to share every waking *moment* with me.

I busy myself organizing the jewelry on my dresser. I reach for Stella's friendship bracelet and quickly slide it into my pocket, afraid that Gracie is going to see it and want to share that, too.

When my stepmom comes back, she dangles something in front of me. It's a necklace—a silver heart pendant on a chain. The pendant must be a hundred

years old, and it's not my style at all. I try not to make a face.

"My grandma gave me this when I was about your age," my stepmom says. "It helped me through a pretty tough time. Try it on and see if you like it."

She places the pendant in my hand and squeezes my shoulder. "Gracie and I are going to do some scrapbooking," she says. "Do you want to join us?"

"Um, not right now," I say, trying not to sound rude.

I catch the flicker of disappointment in my stepmom's eyes. "Maybe later," she says, closing the door gently behind her.

Turn to page 4.

4

As quiet settles over the room, I check the clock. 3:52. I wonder what Stella's doing right now.

I sigh, stretch out on the bed, and examine the pendant. It has a hinge along the left side of the heart. Is it a locket? I slide my thumbnail down the groove on the other side and try to open the locket. It won't budge.

I reach for a nail file and try to pry the locket open. Just as I'm about to give up, I hear a *pop*. The now-open locket springs from my hand and disappears over the edge of the bed.

Scooting forward on my stomach, I peer over the side of the bed and reach for the locket. It's empty—no photos, no secret messages, no nothing. But as my fingers close around the locket, I feel my stomach drop. Something shifts beneath me, and then I'm falling. I squeeze my eyes shut, bracing for impact. I wait—one second, two, three—much too long for such a short fall. When my body finally hits the floor, I feel a sharp pain in my temple. *Ouch!* Did I hit the dresser?

As I reach for my forehead, my hand brushes against something rough—not carpet, but something strangely familiar: grass. I open my eyes to a field of

green, blinking against the blinding sunlight.

My temple is throbbing as I try to sit up. The world spins slowly around me in a colorful haze. I take a deep, steadying breath, a breath filled with the scent of lilacs. I glance over my shoulder at a long row of green bushes bursting with purple flowers. I'm sitting beside a lilac hedge on a broad lawn. Behind me, a tunnel through the hedge leads to another yard. Across the lawn is the back of an enormous gray house, several stories tall with a tower on top. As I gaze upward, I start to get dizzy.

I reach for a large rock beside the lilac hedge and take a few more breaths to steady myself. A minute passes, maybe two. Gazing down at the ground, I try to remember how I got here. I was on the bed, staring down at the locket on the floor. I fell and hit my head, but on what? This rock?

Something glitters in the grass beside me. It's the necklace from my stepmom, sunlight dancing across the engraved face of the heart-shaped pendant. It seems shinier than I remember. I reach for the locket. As my fingers close around it, the hinge clicks and the locket snaps shut.

The locket *is* shinier than it was before, and this time, when I slide my thumbnail along the edge, it pops open smoothly. That's when I feel the now-familiar sensation of the ground dropping away from beneath me. I squeeze my eyes shut and hold my breath.

The landing is much softer this time. I lie still, afraid to open my eyes. But as I rub my fingertips along the ground, I feel soft carpet.

My eyes fly open, and I'm relieved to see the edge of a pink bedspread dangling just inches from my face. I'm on the floor, my hand clenched around the locket.

Sitting up, I check the clock on the nightstand. 3:52. No time has passed since I first opened the locket on my bed. Did I fall asleep for a few seconds? Was I dreaming? The bump on my forehead says no, but maybe I hit the dresser when I fell out of bed.

Am I awake *now*? I pinch the skin on my arm and wince at the sting. Yup, definitely awake. I glance at the door, and then back at the necklace. Part of me is afraid to open the locket again. The other part of me can't *not* open it, especially now that I know I can get back to my room when I want to—or need to—and that no one will miss me while I'm gone.

7

My heart flutters with excitement. As I force open the locket and close my eyes, I think, *If only Stella were here, too . . .*

Turn to page 8.

I hear the snapping of branches and feel a sharp scrape against my ankle. I open my eyes wide and find myself surrounded by a web of branches and the sweet smell of flowers. This time I've landed in the tunnel of the lilac bushes that connects the yard of the gray house to the yard of the house next door. But where's my locket? I almost panic, until I realize that I'm clutching it in my fist.

Suddenly I hear the *creak* of a door hinge and voices. I crawl forward through the tunnel and peer through the leaves at the gray house. A sour-faced woman steps onto the porch, a broom in her hand and a rolled-up rug resting on her hip. She's wearing a long, old-fashioned skirt and apron, and her brown hair is pulled back into a tight little bun. Behind her, a dark-haired girl skips out onto the porch and down the steps into the backyard. When I see what she's wearing, I suck in my breath. Her fancy pink dress has delicate lace trim, and her wide sash is tied in an enormous bow. These two seem to have walked straight out of the pages of a history book.

As the girl takes a few steps into the yard, my heart races. She's walking right toward me. I shrink back into

the tunnel, not sure if I want her to see me or not.

Whap, whap, whap! A thumping sound makes me jump. Across the yard, the woman with the bun has tossed her rug over a clothesline and is whacking it with the broom. Wouldn't a vacuum cleaner be easier?

I glance quickly forward again, looking for the dark-haired girl. Suddenly she pops into view, perched on the edge of a wooden swing hanging from a tree branch. She can't be more than three feet away. She looks friendly and curious, her brown eyes shining. *Who is she?* I wonder. *Why is she dressed like that?* She looks like someone I'd like to meet, someone with an interesting story to tell.

Suddenly, there's a sharp tug on my foot. Someone—or some *thing*—is trying to pull me backward into the tunnel!

I yelp, yank my foot away, and scramble out of the hedge. I whirl around to get a good look at my attacker— a redheaded boy with a snub-nosed face. He's on his hands and knees, peering through the tunnel from the yard next door.

"Hey!" he says in an accusatory tone. "What were you doing in there?"

My skin bristles. "I was looking for something," I shoot back in a tone that says "none of your business."

"Oh, yeah?" he says, crawling through the hole after me. "Looking for what?" He's trying to sound tough, but it's hard to take him seriously in his knee-length pants and bow tie. His clothes look as outdated as the dark-haired girl's, and also kind of silly. I'm not the slightest bit scared of this boy.

"I was looking for *this*," I say, dangling the locket from my hand.

The boy seems intrigued by my locket—too intrigued. He grabs the locket for a closer look.

When I see my locket—my way back home—in someone else's hands, I start to worry. "Hey!" I say to the boy. "That's mine!"

"Eddie!" the dark-haired girl shouts, running over to us. "You give that back right now!" she orders, her hands on her hips. The friendliness I saw in her face moments ago has vanished. She looks fierce.

Eddie drops the locket into my outstretched hand, sticks out his tongue at the girl, and scurries back through the tunnel.

"What's all that nonsense about, Samantha?"

the woman with the broom calls from behind us.

Now I know the girl's name: *Samantha.*

Before answering the woman, Samantha cocks her head at me curiously and reaches out a hand to help me up. "Everything's all right!" she calls back. "I just, um, stumbled upon a friend." She smiles warmly, and I can't help but smile back.

Samantha's eyes flicker with surprise as she takes in my outfit. I glance down, too, and notice for the first time the grass stains on the knees of my tan capris. My tennis shoes are untied, and there's a thin stream of blood trickling down my ankle from where the lilac bush scratched me. I tug a twig from my hair and feel my cheeks flush hot.

Samantha must see how embarrassed I am, because she gives me another reassuring smile. "I'm Samantha Parkington," she says. Then she tucks one leg behind the other and dips into a curtsy, the way girls did a very long time ago.

I fight the urge to curtsy back, because I'm not sure I know how. Instead, I nod my head awkwardly. Then I ask politely, "Is that your mother?" I point toward the woman beating the rug with the broom.

Samantha giggles. "No!" she says, loudly enough to cause the woman to glance in our direction. "That's Elsa. She's the maid."

Maid? I've never met someone who had an actual maid before. Are Samantha's parents rich?

When I fall silent, Samantha keeps talking, as if she's afraid the conversation will end. "I don't have a mother, actually," she says. "My parents died when I was little. I live here with Grandmary—that is, my grandmother."

My stomach clenches at those words. Samantha's parents died? "I'm sorry" is all I can say.

"I don't remember them very well," she says, looking away. "I was only five when they died." Samantha pauses before she turns back to me. "I'm very lucky to be able to live here with Grandmary."

I glance at the enormous house behind Samantha. "Your house is really beautiful. You must have lots of space." I think about the cramped room I share with Gracie. I'd give anything for a little space right now.

Samantha stares at the house thoughtfully. "Sometimes *too* much space," she says. "It gets lonely, especially since school got out. I haven't seen a girl my

age in, well, *ages*—I mean, until now." She smiles again.

Suddenly Samantha's expression changes, and I get the distinct feeling that someone is standing behind me.

Turn to page 14.

It's Elsa. She's wearing a scowl—which turns to confusion as her eyes travel down to my dirty capris. "Do I know you, miss?" she asks.

I shake my head. "I don't think so," I mumble.

"Where are you from?" she persists.

I don't have my father's address memorized yet. "I'm . . . um, from the city . . . ma'am."

Realization dawns on Elsa's pinched face. "Ah," she says. "You must be Ruby—the laundry girl we sent for from the city. But Mrs. Edwards wasn't expecting you till summer's end! I've got enough work this week preparing for our trip to Piney Point. The last thing I need is to be looking after a new girl."

Laundry girl? Does Elsa think I'm some kind of servant?

Samantha sees my hesitation. "Wait, Elsa, I'm not sure that this girl *is* Ruby. I think she was just out riding her bicycle. Isn't that right?" she asks me.

I can't answer Samantha—I'm too confused. Why does she think I was riding a bike?

"See? She's wearing bloomers," Samantha says to Elsa, pointing at my capris. She turns to me. "I wish I could learn to ride, too, but . . . I'm afraid Grandmary

thinks bloomers and bicycles aren't very ladylike."

"Well?" says Elsa. "Which is it, miss? Are you Ruby, come here from the city to help with the wash? Or were you just out riding one of those frightful bicycle contraptions?"

I glance at Samantha. Her cheeks are flushed pink, and her smile is friendly—and curious. She seems excited to have me here, and the truth is, I'm excited, too, to get to know her better. And I'd love to see the inside of her beautiful house! If I tell Elsa that I'm the laundry girl, I might get to do that. On the other hand, I don't know much about doing laundry.

Elsa crosses her arms, waiting for my response.

To tell Elsa that I'm Ruby, the laundry girl, turn to page 26.

To tell Elsa that I'm not Ruby, turn to page 21.

Grandmary introduces herself to me as Mrs. Edwards. She eyes me up and down, as if she disapproves of my outfit, and I flush with embarrassment as I did when I first met Samantha. But there's kindness in Grandmary's blue-gray eyes, and a hint of curiosity, too.

Hawkins returns to the kitchen and tells Grandmary that he'll phone the doctor. He reaches for a large wooden box on the wall beside the sink and lifts something that looks like a small trumpet to his ear. Then he cranks a little handle on the side of the box, and in a moment he's speaking into another trumpet-shaped piece on the front of the box. *That's* the telephone?

When I hear Hawkins asking for the doctor, I feel another swell of anxiety. I rub the heart-shaped pendant in my pocket, reminding myself that I can go home anytime I want.

"Yes. Oh, yes, I see," says Hawkins. When he hangs up, he looks concerned. "Mrs. Edwards, ma'am," he says to Grandmary, "the doctor is busy with other patients this afternoon. He invites us to come to his office and wait, or if we prefer, he will attempt to make

a house call later this evening."

Grandmary studies me, as if wondering how critical my condition is. I'm not sick, am I? Maybe I *did* bump my head too hard. That would definitely explain a lot.

To insist that all is well,
turn to page 34.

To agree to go to the doctor's office,
turn to page 40.

I nod yes to Samantha's question. I'm definitely on my own.

Elsa snorts. "An orphan?" she says. "Well, that's not what we requested."

Wait, she thinks I'm an orphan? That's not what I meant by "on my own," but now it's too late. Everything is happening so fast, and I can't keep up.

"Surely we should send her back, ma'am," Elsa blurts to Mrs. Edwards. "We requested a servant—a hard worker—not some parentless child to care for."

Samantha steps up beside me. I see the steely look in her eyes, much like her grandmother's, when she says, "It's not Ruby's fault that she's an orphan." She grasps my hand as if to say, *You're not alone. I'm here with you.*

Mrs. Edwards lifts her hand to silence Elsa. "That's quite enough, Elsa," she says. "Ruby has suffered some misfortune, but she's not to blame for that. I'm sure she'll be a hard worker. Now do as I ask and show her to her room."

Samantha reluctantly lets go of my hand, but not before whispering, "I'll see you in a little while."

Elsa casts a sharp look at me as she leads me out

of the parlor. We go through the kitchen and up a long, curving staircase. Then we start up a narrower set of stairs to the third floor. Elsa moves surprisingly quickly—as if hoping to lose me around the next bend. I hurry down the hall after her.

Elsa points out two closed doors. The first is her room, and the second is where Jessie, Mrs. Edwards's seamstress, works.

At the end of the hall, Elsa starts up another staircase. These stairs are steeper than the rest. As I hurry after Elsa, I'm out of breath but eager to see the room above. It must be in the tower that I noticed when I first landed in Samantha's backyard.

The staircase leads to a small but sunny room lined with big windows. There's no bed or furniture of any kind in the room. Obviously Mrs. Edwards wasn't expecting me—or Ruby—anytime soon.

Now that we've reached our destination, Elsa finally stands still. She puts her hands on her hips and says sternly, "Listen now, Ruby. Mrs. Edwards will be counting on me to make sure you earn your keep. You'll need to prove that you can work hard, or you'll be sent back. Do you understand?"

She puts a finger under my chin and lifts my face so that I'm looking straight into her narrowed eyes. "Do you understand?" she asks again.

I try to nod, but Elsa still has ahold of my face. "Yes," I say finally.

"Yes, *ma'am,*" Elsa corrects me. "We'll have to work on your manners. Now stay here while I find you some proper clothes to wear."

When I'm alone, my first urge is to pull the pendant out of my pocket and go home. Then I remember how Samantha stood by me when she thought I was feeling all alone, and what she said about sometimes feeling lonely herself in this big house. I think of my bedroom at my dad's, which feels lonely now, too. I'd rather stay here with my new friend. *You can handle grumpy Elsa,* I tell myself, *at least with Samantha by your side.*

I fasten the locket firmly around my neck.

Turn to page 42.

"Um, I'm—I'm sorry, but I'm not Ruby," I stammer.

Elsa leans forward and says, "Well, then, miss, you'd better explain what you're doing here in Mrs. Edwards's hedge, looking like something the cat dragged in."

Samantha winces at Elsa's words. "Actually, I think you look quite nice in your bloomers," she says, lifting her chin slightly. "But where's your bicycle?" she asks, glancing toward the hedge.

I follow her eyes toward the hedge, as if my bicycle might somehow magically appear there.

"Jiminy, look at the bump on the side of your head!" Samantha exclaims. "Did you crash?"

Even Elsa's face softens as she examines my head, which has started to throb. "Sakes alive," she whispers, "that's a goose egg if I ever saw one. Let's take you inside, miss, and let Mrs. Hawkins have a look."

This time, I don't argue. I'm feeling kind of dizzy. I follow Elsa up the steps of the porch and through the back door, feeling Samantha close on my heels.

The door leads into a warm, spacious kitchen, with cupboards to my left and a sink and stove to my right.

When I see the stove, I do a double take. It's bright blue and looks like an antique. So does the long black dress of the plump, white-haired woman who turns from the stove to greet me. This must be Mrs. Hawkins.

"Merciful heavens!" Mrs. Hawkins says when she sees me, my hand pressed to my head. "Sit down, child."

As Mrs. Hawkins fills a bowl with water from the sink, I sit in a wooden chair and glance at the newspaper resting on the table beside me. "Record Crowds Enjoy World's Fair in St. Louis," the headline blares. I lift the front page to read the date at the top: *June 1, 1904.*

Turn to page 28.

I try to focus on the question at hand. "My family . . . is in the city," I say to Samantha. "And yes, Mrs. Edwards, a dollar a week sounds just fine."

Mrs. Edwards nods and then signals Elsa to take me to my room. Elsa purses her lips and doesn't say a word as she leads me—quickly—up several flights of stairs, each narrower than the first, to a tiny room. Is this the tower room I noticed from the yard outside?

When Elsa tells me to wait here while she gathers some clothing for me, I'm happy to do it. I need a minute to try to figure out if I made the right decision. *Wash girl? What do I know about doing the laundry?* I wonder.

Then I think of Samantha, who seems so eager to have a friend to spend time with. Wasn't I just hoping for the same thing, sitting at my dad's, missing my friend Stella?

If I stay here for a while, maybe Samantha can help me with the laundry and we'll have time left over to have some fun together. Besides, I can go home any-time I want.

When Elsa returns, she hands me a drab gray dress

and apron. I can tell by looking at it that the dress is too big, but Elsa doesn't seem to notice. "Try it on," she barks as she crosses her arms and turns her back to give me some privacy.

I take off my capris and T-shirt and step into the dress, feeling the rough material scratch against my skin. I turn in a circle so that Elsa can inspect the dress, which comes almost to my ankles. "It'll have to do," she says with a sigh. "Now fold those bloomers and let's set you to work."

As Elsa heads to the stairs, I fold my clothes and leave them in a neat pile on the floor. I'm about to leave the room when I suddenly remember my locket. Where is it? Still in my capris, I hope. I hurry back to my clothes, reach for the folded pants, and slide my hand into the pocket. I breathe a sigh of relief when I feel the heart-shaped pendant. As I slip the chain around my neck, I try to ignore the impatient look on Elsa's face. Then I hurry to rejoin her on the stairs.

Turn to page 36.

I count to ten, slowly, before responding to Eddie—and that gives Samantha just enough time to hurl her own response at him. "Eddie Ryland," she says, "you get out of here *right* now or I'll tell your mother that you dumped out one of her expensive bottles of perfume to make a house for your pet beetles. Don't think I won't!"

Eddie jumps up, staring at Samantha as if to see whether she's bluffing. Then he slinks back through the hedge like a dog with its tail between its legs. Samantha has clearly had her share of arguments with Eddie. I'm glad I let her handle this one.

"Thanks," I say to Samantha. But as we keep working side by side, I remember what Eddie asked her: *Why are you helping that servant girl?*

Turn to page 52.

can do the wash," I say to Elsa. *At least I'll try,* I think to myself.

Elsa reaches for my elbow. "Well, come along then," she says. "Let's introduce you to Mrs. Edwards."

I follow Elsa across the backyard and into the house. When I glance back at Samantha, she gives me a reassuring smile.

We step into the kitchen, where a white-haired woman is stirring something in a pot on a bright blue stove. When Elsa introduces her as Mrs. Hawkins, the cook, she turns to smile kindly at me. She, too, wears a starched white apron and a black dress that reaches to the floor.

I glance around the spacious kitchen, sensing that something is missing. That's when it hits me—there's no dishwasher. There's no microwave. There's not even a refrigerator!

Elsa turns to see why I'm not following her. "Come along, girl," she says impatiently. "Mrs. Edwards is in the parlor."

Elsa leads me down the hall and into a fancy room where I see an elegant silver-haired woman writing a letter at a small desk. Is this Samantha's grandmother?

"Mrs. Edwards, ma'am," says Elsa, clearing her throat politely.

The woman glances up, her pen poised. "Yes, Elsa?" she says. Her steel-gray eyes flicker over to me, and then back to Elsa.

"Our wash girl, Ruby, arrived early from the city," says Elsa. "There's been some misunderstanding. Shall I send her back, ma'am?"

As Mrs. Edwards looks me up and down, casting a distinct look of disapproval at my outfit, I wish I could blend into the rose-patterned walls behind me.

Turn to page 32.

There's a rushing sound in my ears, like ocean waves. *1904?* I press my fingertips against my throbbing forehead. Did I fall out of bed and fall backward in *time*? That would explain the old-fashioned stove and the odd, antique-looking clothes that everyone here is wearing.

Mrs. Hawkins sets the bowl of water on the table. "Dear me, that's a nasty bump, isn't it?" she says, tilting my chin upward so that she can examine my head. "What happened, love?"

"She fell off her bicycle," says Samantha, who is hovering over my shoulder.

Mrs. Hawkins *tsk-tsks*. "All right, Samantha," she says. "Step back now so that I can clean up this child." As Mrs. Hawkins presses a cold, wet cloth to my head, she asks, "Where do you live, dear?"

"She's from the city," Samantha answers for me. "Did you take the train here to Mount Bedford? Surely you didn't ride your bicycle!"

I stare at my feet, wondering how to answer that question. "To be honest," I say, "I'm not exactly sure how I got here. Everything was kind of a blur."

There's a stretch of silence. When I glance up,

Samantha looks worried, and Mrs. Hawkins places her hand against my forehead, as if checking my temperature. "Samantha, run along and find Mr. Hawkins for me, will you, dear?" she says in an overly cheery tone of voice.

Samantha jumps up from her chair obediently, casts one last anxious look in my direction, and then darts down the hall.

Mrs. Hawkins pats my leg and tells me she'll make an ice pack for my head. Then she opens one side of a large wooden cabinet. It must be some kind of refrigerator because there's food and bottles of milk inside. On the top of the compartment is an enormous block of ice. Mrs. Hawkins chips away at the ice with a sharp pick and puts the pieces in a linen towel.

Moments later, a balding man in a black suit appears with Samantha close behind. He says under his breath to Mrs. Hawkins, "Shall I call the doctor?"

The doctor? "I'm really okay—" I start to say, but Mrs. Hawkins interrupts me.

"It's probably nothing, dear," she says, "but it doesn't hurt to let the doctor have a look." She turns to the man. "Before you call the doctor, would you let

Mrs. Edwards know of our young guest?"

The man nods and leaves the kitchen, and Mrs. Hawkins hands me the ice pack. "Hold that to your head, dear," she says kindly. "Just sit and rest for a few moments. That will do you a world of good." Mrs. Hawkins pats my shoulder and then goes back to the stove to stir whatever is bubbling inside the large pot.

Samantha pulls her chair closer to mine and sits down, hugging her knees to her chest. "That was Hawkins, our butler," she whispers, as if making conversation to take my mind off the doctor's visit. "He's married to Mrs. Hawkins. They live in the room above the carriage house."

A butler *and* a cook? And they *live* here? Wow, Samantha's grandmother sure must have a lot of money. I've always wondered what that would be like.

Samantha suddenly jumps back up from her chair. An elegant silver-haired woman walks into the kitchen in a long blue skirt and jacket.

"Good afternoon, Samantha," the woman says.

"Good afternoon, Grandmary," Samantha says with a graceful curtsy. She glances nervously at me and bobs her head upward, as if reminding me to

mind my manners, too. I stand up and try to imitate Samantha by tucking one grass-stained knee behind the other. I've never curtsied before, and I feel like an awkward mess next to Samantha and her elegant grandmother.

Turn to page 16.

It's Samantha who pipes up from the doorway and rescues me. "Excuse me, Grandmary," she says politely, "but Ruby must be tired from her trip to Mount Bedford. May she stay with us tonight?"

Mrs. Edwards seems surprised to hear from Samantha, but her eyes are kind when she says, "Yes, I suspect Ruby *is* tired from her journey. She'll stay with us tonight and help with preparations for Piney Point tomorrow. If all goes well, she can join us on our trip. Elsa, please show Ruby to her room and find her some proper clothing."

Elsa's face darkens. She starts to lead me away, reluctantly, when Mrs. Edwards says, "Wait. Before you go, Ruby, let's discuss your wages. If you stay with us, I'll pay you a dollar a week for your service. Will that be acceptable to your family?"

A dollar a week? I get much more than that for my allowance, and that's just for doing a few chores. I'm trying not to make a face when I notice the calendar on the wall above the desk. The year at the top reads 1904.

1904? I do a double take, but the numbers are crystal clear. Did I just open a locket and travel back in time more than a *hundred years*?

My head starts spinning again, and I reach for the frame of the doorway to steady myself.

When I don't answer Mrs. Edwards's question about my family, Samantha leans forward and asks gently, "Are you on your own, Ruby?"

At the moment, I do feel alone—and very confused.

To nod yes,
turn to page 18.

To say something about my family,
turn to page 23.

I tell Grandmary that I'd really rather not go to the doctor's office—that I'm feeling much better now.

She hesitates but says, "Very well. Let's rest in the parlor for a time and then reassess the situation." Relief washes over me as I follow Grandmary and Samantha out the kitchen door and down the hall.

The parlor is so elegant that I'm afraid to step into it with my dirty tennis shoes and capris. The walls are lined with plush red velvet chairs. Large windows framed with red curtains open up onto the front porch.

"Lie here, dear," says Grandmary, patting a small sofa. I lie back against a lacy pillow. I try to relax, but it's difficult when Samantha keeps staring at me from a chair nearby.

"Oh, good heavens," Grandmary mutters. "I nearly forgot about our dinner party. I had better send Hawkins next door to reschedule with the Rylands." She reaches for a shiny gold rope on the wall and gives it a quick tug.

Moments later, Hawkins appears. When Grandmary asks him to cancel plans with the Rylands, he nods and then asks, "Shall I send in Mrs. Hawkins,

ma'am, to discuss alternate dinner plans?"

"No, no," Grandmary replies. "I'll speak with her myself. Samantha, would you please look after our guest—quietly—while I'm gone?"

Samantha nods eagerly. I can almost see the wheels in her head turning, as if she's trying to figure out what "quiet" fun we can have. "Would you like to see a magic lantern show?" she asks.

Turn to page 43.

36

I expect to be shown to a washing machine in the basement. Instead, Elsa leads me to the backyard, where clothes are soaking in a big tub.

"Soap the clothes and scrub them on the washboard," Elsa orders.

On a *what*? Elsa hands me a long metal tray with ridges. She lays a piece of wet clothing over the washboard, showing me how to gently squeeze and rub the clothing against the ridged tray. "These are Mrs. Edwards's dresses," Elsa cautions, "so make sure you get them clean—carefully."

The long dresses are dark and heavy with water. Are there stains on the clothing? I can't tell, so I do my best to scrub every inch. One by one, I scrub the dresses and move them to a second tub, which Elsa refills now and then with hot water from the stove in the kitchen.

Elsa keeps checking up on me, as if she thinks I'm going to mess up. When she finally announces that we're done with the washing, I'm thrilled. I'm exhausted, my shoulders ache, and I'm hungry. But then Elsa says it's time to *rinse* the clothes and hang them out to dry. Ugh.

Elsa teaches me how to crank the wet clothes through a "wringer," a wooden frame with two wide rollers. Afterward, I'm hanging the still-damp clothes on the clothesline when the porch door swings open and out pops Samantha.

"There you are!" she says. "May I help?"

I nod eagerly. This is what I was hoping for—that Samantha and I could spend some time together. She hums as she lifts a dress from the washtub.

"It'll be fun working together, won't it?" she asks, as if reading my mind. "I don't have any chores of my own to do."

No chores? Even at my dad's house, I have chores to do. I picture the chore chart taped to his refrigerator. I wasn't very happy when I first saw it, but Dad said I'm a part of the family, so I need to pitch in, too.

I glimpse Samantha's face as she helps me with the wash. She really does look as if she's having fun. Maybe after a while, you get bored with servants doing all of your work for you.

I have a feeling Elsa won't let *me* get bored today. I reach for another piece of clothing.

A few minutes later, annoying Eddie from next

door appears in the hole in the hedge. "What are you doing helping that *servant* girl?" he asks Samantha. "You'd better not let your grandmother see you."

Eddie says "servant" as if it's a bad thing. I'm not really a servant, but if I were, I wouldn't want to be treated this way. I feel my face grow hot.

Samantha lifts her chin and reaches for another piece of clothing. "Her *name* is Ruby," she snaps at him. "And never you mind what I'm doing. Worry about your own self, Eddie Ryland."

Eddie doesn't respond, but he sits down cross-legged beside the hedge and watches us. When I lean forward to lift more laundry from the tub, my locket dangles before me, catching Eddie's eye.

"So where'd you get that necklace?" Eddie asks me. "Did you steal it?"

Steal it? This boy is out of control.

"I didn't *steal* anything," I say to Eddie. "This necklace was a gift from my . . ." I pause, not sure if I should use the word "stepmom." Would it be easier just to call her my mother?

I must pause too long, and Eddie takes my hesitation as proof that I'm a thief.

"You *stole* it," he says, pointing his finger at me. "I know you did, because no ragbag like you would have a necklace as nice as that."

A hot wave of anger brings tears to my eyes, but there's no way I'm going to let this kid see me cry. My fingers tighten on the wet skirt in my hands.

To lash out at Eddie, turn to page 45.

To count to ten instead, turn to page 25.

As soon as I agree to go to the doctor's office, my heart starts racing. Samantha sees the look on my face and says, "Don't be frightened. Dr. Barnett is very nice. I'll stay with you the whole time if you'd like."

I nod gratefully.

Hawkins has called us a cab, but there's no yellow taxi waiting in front of the house. Instead, a horse-drawn carriage is *clip-clopping* toward us. I suddenly feel very far away from home.

As the driver stops in front of the house, Samantha links her arm with mine and leads me up to the carriage. The tall white horse swishes its tail and stamps its foot, as if telling me to hurry along.

Hawkins helps me up into the carriage seat, and then Samantha and Grandmary step up behind me. The driver clucks his tongue, and the horse begins walking, then trotting. As we bounce and sway down the street, I see other horse-drawn carriages, along with a very odd-looking car up ahead.

The shiny black car has large narrow wheels, no roof, and just a single seat. It looks like the antique cars I've seen in parades back home. A man is vigorously

cranking a handle on the front of the car. As we draw near the car, I hear a loud *clank,* and then the rumble of the motor. The sound is deafening—somewhere between a lawn mower and a motorcycle. The whole car shakes.

As the man drives the car away from the curb, bucking and lurching forward, Samantha turns to me and asks sweetly, "Does the noise hurt your head?"

When I shake my head no, Samantha says proudly, "My uncle Gard has an automobile. I can't wait to ride in it!"

Grandmary seems less enthusiastic. "Those modern machines are such a nuisance," she mutters, lifting a gloved hand to cover her ear.

Modern machines? I stifle a giggle, imagining what Grandmary would think of cars in my time, a hundred years from now. They're quieter, yes, but there sure are a lot more of them.

Turn to page 46.

Elsa returns with some blankets and a drab gray dress and apron. She insists that I put the clothes on right away. When I step into the dress, the rough material chafes my skin. It feels like a burlap sack.

I try not to squirm as Elsa inspects me. "It'll have to do," she says. Then she crosses her arms. "Now, tell the truth, Ruby. Have you worked as a wash girl before?"

I think of the one time my mom let me do laundry and wonder if that counts.

When I take too long to answer, Elsa scoffs and shakes her head. "We'll have to find other ways to make you useful, then," she says. She starts down the stairs, waving me to follow. "We're having a dinner party this evening, and that dining table must be the picture of perfection. Shall we start with the table settings or the napkin folding?"

To help with setting the table, turn to page 48.

To help with folding the napkins, turn to page 57.

Samantha pulls the curtains closed and fiddles with the "magic lantern," a metal box with two tubes extending from the front. A soft light glows within the box, projecting an image onto the wall. It's a painting of an Eskimo in a sled.

As Samantha shows me more images of far-away places, it occurs to me that this lantern isn't very "magical." *What would Samantha think of TVs, computers, and cell phones?* I wonder, wishing I had my mom's tablet with me so that I could download a movie for Samantha.

"I'd like to visit *all* of these places," she says wistfully, "but I've never been farther away than Piney Point. That's our summer home in the mountains, where we'll be going the day after tomorrow."

When Samantha flips to an image of the Grand Canyon, I say, "I've been there!"

Samantha's jaw drops. "Really?" she says. "Jeepers, you wear bloomers and ride bicycles and travel to faraway places. I haven't done any of those things."

"So you don't have a bicycle?" I ask. I remember then what Samantha told me when we first met—that

she'd never learned to ride a bicycle.

Samantha shrugs. "There's one in the shed that belonged to my uncle Gard," she says, "but Grandmary won't let me ride it. She thinks bicycles are much too dangerous."

Turn to page 49.

I ball up the skirt in my hands and whip it at Eddie, just narrowly missing his head. He ducks and starts squawking, which brings Elsa running out the back door.

After listening to Eddie's side of the story, Elsa gives *me* a major scolding. She reminds me to keep my place. "He may be just a boy, and sometimes a rude boy at that," she says, "but he's Master Eddie to you. You will show him respect. Do you understand?"

Respect? I swallow hard. Doing the laundry this afternoon was tough. Respecting Eddie is going to be even tougher.

Samantha leans against the oak tree while I get my scolding. She kicks at the ground with her toe, glancing at me with sad, apologetic eyes. When Elsa goes back into the house, Samantha is right there beside me again.

"I'm sorry, Ruby," she says. She casts a somewhat nervous look back at the house and then reaches down to lift another piece of clothing from the tub.

Turn to page 52.

I'm surprised when the cab stops in front of a small cream-colored house. Are we picking up someone else? But when the driver reaches for my hand to help me down, I realize this must be the doctor's office. Yikes. What kind of a doctor works out of his home? My stomach clenches.

Grandmary leads the way up the porch steps, and she walks through the front door without knocking, as if the home were her own. Two people are waiting in what looks like a living room: a man with a bandaged foot and a pair of crutches, and a small girl with red blisters all over her face. *What's wrong with her?*

As I settle onto a leather couch beside Samantha, I glance again at the little girl. She's scratching her palms now. There must be itchy blisters there, too. I try to avoid looking at the girl, but Samantha leans toward her and says, "You must have chicken pox. Does it itch terribly?" When the girl nods, Samantha says reassuringly, "It'll get better soon. Don't worry."

Grandmary says to me in a low voice, "Samantha and I have already had the chicken pox. Have you had it, too, dear, I hope?"

I shake my head no. "I don't think so," I say. I'm

pretty sure I'd remember something like that.

"Is it contagious?" I ask with alarm.

Grandmary nods. "It is, indeed."

As I steal another glance at the girl, Samantha reaches for my hand. We sit in silence, counting the seconds along with the grandfather clock in the corner. The girl coughs without covering her mouth. I glance nervously at Samantha and sink lower into my seat.

"It'll be all right," she says warmly. "You'll see."

Turn to page 53.

Setting the table will be a piece of cake—I've done it a gazillion times. But when Elsa opens the cabinet in the dining room, I'm terrified to touch the dishes. The china plates are even fancier than the ones my grandmother uses for Thanksgiving!

When I've carefully set a plate in front of each chair, I breathe a sigh of relief. Then I open the silverware drawer. I'm stumped. There are forks, knives, and spoons of all shapes and sizes. Which ones do I use? I make my best guess and arrange the utensils next to the plates. Then I stand back to admire my work.

"Ruby, where is your head?" Elsa squawks as she steps back into the room. "We're serving a *formal* dinner. This won't do."

She pulls out more silverware and does some fancy rearranging, explaining where the fish, meat, and salad forks should go. "And you forgot the soup spoons. And the salt spoons," she adds, reaching for a set of tiny spoons.

When the table is set properly, Elsa sets about finding me something *else* to do.

Turn to page 69.

Samantha and I flip through a few more magic lantern pictures before Grandmary returns to ask how I'm feeling.

"Much better," I assure her.

Grandmary raises an eyebrow, not quite convinced. I'm going to have to try harder if I have any hope of avoiding a doctor's visit.

I sit up—just to show Grandmary that I can—and add, "I remember where I was going, actually." Out of the corner of my eye, I see Samantha's eyes widen with interest. "My mother put me on a train at Grand Central Station in the city. I was traveling to Plattsburgh to stay with family for the summer, but then I . . . hit my head and—"

"Plattsburgh?" Samantha interrupts. "That sounds so familiar." She chews her lip thoughtfully.

"It's not too far from Piney Point, Samantha," says Grandmary. "We'll see 'Plattsburgh' on the train schedule when we travel to Piney Point this week."

Samantha bolts upright and says, "Oh, I just had the most *wonderful* idea. Maybe you could stay with us at Piney Point for a day or two before going on to visit your relatives in Plattsburgh! We could swim, and

hike, and pick wildflowers . . . oh, Grandmary, may she come?"

I have to admit—Piney Point *does* sound like fun. And if I go, I can stay with Samantha for a few more days and get to know her better. But what will Grandmary say?

"Please, Grandmary," Samantha begs. "I've never had a friend come with me to Piney Point before. I can't imagine anything more wonderful!"

Grandmary's face softens, and I know her answer even before she says the words. But she insists that I telephone my family to ask permission. "You must try," she says firmly. "I'm sure they're worried about you."

I know I won't be able to reach my dad by phone, but I have to follow Grandmary's orders and try. Back in the kitchen, Mrs. Hawkins shows me how to crank the handle on the side of the phone box and hold the receiver to my ear. Then she hurries into the dining room to make sure Elsa has set the table.

When I hear the operator's voice, I ask her about listings in Plattsburgh under my dad's name. Suddenly the line gets disconnected. "Hello?" I say. "Hello?"

"Hang up and try again," Samantha urges. I replace

the receiver, and the telephone suddenly rings: two short rings and one long. "Answer it!" Samantha says quickly. "That's our ring. We share a party line with the neighbors, but that call is for us."

I lift the receiver and hear the operator saying that she has no listings under my dad's name.

I thank the operator for her help, but before I hang up the phone, I catch a glimpse of Samantha's face. She's covering her mouth with her hands as if holding her breath, her eyes filled with hope. How can I let her down?

Turn to page 59.

"Are you sure you should be helping me?" I ask Samantha. "I don't want you to get into trouble."

"Oh, it's all right," Samantha assures me. "You don't know how long I've been waiting for you—a girl my own age—to come to this house. It's . . . well, sometimes it gets really lonely without sisters or brothers." As she slides a clothespin over the wet sleeve of a dress, she asks, "Do you have any sisters or brothers?"

I think of my stepsister Gracie only briefly before shaking my head no.

"See, then, it's perfect!" says Samantha. "You belong here, Ruby. It'll be like we're sisters. We can work together, play together, and—"

"Samantha!" Mrs. Edwards's voice pierces the air from the back door. "Whatever are you doing out here? Come inside and change your clothes for dinner."

Samantha's face falls, so I try to lift her spirits with a joke. "And we can get into *trouble* together," I whisper. It works—Samantha grins at me before hurrying toward the house.

Turn to page 61.

When the door to the doctor's office swings open, I jump. A woman with a long white apron walks out, leading a young boy and his mother. The boy has even more blisters than the girl in the waiting room. I can see some on his swollen eyelids.

"This menthol salve will help with the itching," says the woman in the apron, handing the mother a small glass jar. "And remember to keep him away from other children as best you can."

The boy walks past me—much too close—as he and his mother leave the waiting room. The little girl hops up and follows them out, casting one last glance over her shoulder at me.

Samantha must see how freaked out I am, because she says, "You won't have to wait much longer for Dr. Barnett to come out."

But it's the woman in the apron who approaches Grandmary. "Good afternoon," she says. "What may I help you with today?"

Grandmary stands and asks, "Are you Dr. Barnett's nurse?"

"Actually," says the woman, "I'm Dr. Annabeth Ross. I'm finishing my final month of training with

Dr. Barnett before starting my own practice."

Grandmary's eyes widen. "Well, we're here to see Dr. Barnett," she says firmly.

Dr. Ross smiles politely. "He's here, too," she says. "Would you follow me, please?"

As we file into the office, Samantha elbows me gently. "A woman doctor!" she breathes. "Can you believe it? Right here in Mount Bedford."

Why is she so surprised? I wonder. My doctor back home is a woman. But I can tell by the disapproving look on Grandmary's face that I won't be seeing the woman doctor today.

The doctor's exam room looks like my dad's cluttered office at home. Framed certificates hang in crooked rows on the walls, and medical books and encyclopedias line the bookshelves. The doctor sits at a wooden desk in the corner, scribbling something on a notepad.

"Ah, good afternoon, Mrs. Edwards," he says, standing to greet us. Instead of a white lab coat, he's wearing a silk vest and dressy pants. The stethoscope around his neck looks familiar, though, and when he pats the top of a leather examination table, I feel

the same rush of anxiety I get every time I go to the doctor's office.

Samantha stands right beside me as I climb onto the table. When the doctor turns on a tall lamp, the light is blinding. I look away, toward a cabinet full of glass vials. When I see a row of sharp-looking instruments in the case, I squeeze my eyes shut. That's when I feel the reassuring warmth of Samantha's hand on my shoulder.

After Grandmary explains to the doctor why we're here, he nods and says, "Yes, bicycle riding can be dangerous indeed." He touches the bump on my head and then pulls a stool over so that he can sit down in front of me. "Dr. Ross, would you please adjust the lamp?"

As the woman doctor moves the lamp closer to the examining table, Samantha watches her every move with fascination. Dr. Barnett asks me to look left and then right as Dr. Ross shines the lamplight into and then away from my eyes.

Next, Dr. Barnett tests my reflexes by tapping just below my knees with a little metal hammer. Then he asks me to hop off the table so that he can test my

strength. I try to hold my arms out to my sides as he pushes down on them, first the left and then the right.

"Good," says the doctor finally, turning toward Grandmary. "I don't see signs of a concussion, but you'll want to keep an eye on her for the next few hours and use ice to reduce the swelling. I'll send some aspirin with you, too, to treat any pain."

Dr. Barnett reaches into his medicine cabinet and selects a glass bottle. As he hands it to Grandmary, she hesitates before taking it.

I hesitate, too, as I follow Grandmary out the front door of the doctor's office and reach backward to pull the door shut behind me. *Did the girl with the chicken pox touch this doorknob?* I wonder. I wipe my sweaty palms on my capris.

Turn to page 63.

Elsa brings me into the kitchen and puts me to work folding big white cloth napkins at the long wooden table. She shows me how to fold each napkin into a fancy shape called a "Bishop's Hat."

My fingers feel clumsy as I fold a napkin in half to form a triangle. I try to fold in the corners and edges as Elsa showed me, but my napkin ends up looking like a paper party hat. Elsa shakes out the napkin and tells me, in an irritated tone, to start again.

When Elsa leaves the room, assuming that I've finally caught on, Mrs. Hawkins casts me a sympathetic glance. She's snipping off the ends of string beans, stopping every now and then to stir a bubbling pot on the stove. She looks as if she has her hands full.

Everything Mrs. Hawkins is preparing smells delicious, but something tells me I won't be enjoying it anytime soon. My stomach rumbles. I should have had another helping of tuna casserole at lunch when my stepmom offered it to me.

Samantha pokes her head into the kitchen. "Hi, Ruby!" she says, snitching a string bean from Mrs. Hawkins, who scolds her playfully.

I look up and smile, happy to see Samantha, but

I don't dare stop working. Who knows when Elsa will come back to check on me.

Samantha plops down beside me and reaches for a napkin. "I'll help," she says. Unfortunately, neither one of us can make anything elegant out of the folded cloth. Samantha's napkin ends up looking like a hot dog.

Mrs. Hawkins shakes her head as if to say she's disappointed in us. But her eyes are smiling when she wipes her hands on her apron and says to me, "Here, love, let me show you."

I hand her my napkin, which turns out to be a big mistake. Elsa steps back into the room just as Mrs. Hawkins is completing a perfect Bishop's Hat—and I'm just sitting there, watching.

"Ruby!" Elsa scolds. "Heaven knows that Mrs. Hawkins has plenty to do without you pestering her. Now let's see if we can find you a job that's more suited to your skills—whatever they may be."

Turn to page 69.

I don't want to disappoint Samantha, so I do the kindest thing I can think of. After I can no longer hear the operator, I pretend to be talking to someone else—a relative who is happy to grant me permission to spend a couple of days at Piney Point. When Samantha hears my words, she starts jumping up and down with excitement.

When I get off the phone, a thrilled Samantha hugs me and then races out onto the back porch. Grandmary is there, overseeing Hawkins's work in the flower garden.

As I step onto the porch behind Samantha, I glance toward the lilac hedge, remembering the first moment I met her there.

Suddenly Eddie's face pokes through the hole in the hedge. He waves his hand at me, beckoning me over. *What does he want?* I wonder. I step off the porch and walk closer.

Before Eddie can say a word, Samantha calls to him, "Go home, Eddie. We're busy here. We're packing for Piney Point."

Grandmary reminds Samantha to mind her manners, but Samantha gives me one of those looks

that says, "Ignore him. He's a big pain."

I'm about to turn away from Eddie when he whispers something that I can't ignore: "I heard you on the telephone," he says. "You're a big *liar*."

Turn to page 68.

When Elsa finally calls *me* inside for dinner, I can hardly wait. I imagine how nice it will be to sit down at a table and eat a meal, even if Elsa is sitting across from me. *Will Samantha eat with us, too?* I wonder.

As it turns out, I have to eat quietly by myself in a corner of the kitchen. Elsa says that Mrs. Edwards is having the Rylands over for dinner.

Wait, the Rylands? I think, my fork paused in midair. *As in Eddie Ryland?*

I strain to hear the voices beyond the swinging door of the kitchen. As I take my last bite of chicken, I hear Mrs. Edwards's voice rising above the others. "It's the strangest thing," she says. "I saw my brooch yesterday. So how did it go missing in less than twenty-four hours?"

Then I hear the annoying voice that I already know too well: Eddie's. "Maybe *she* took it—that new servant girl," he says. "I think she's been stealing things."

Anger ignites in my chest, and I suddenly can't swallow my food.

A woman hushes Eddie, and then Elsa bursts through the swinging door carrying dishes. As she sets the dishes in the sink, she asks me quietly and curtly if

I've seen Mrs. Edwards's dragonfly brooch.

I shake my head firmly. Elsa considers my response with a sour look on her face. Then she glances at my empty plate and tells me it's time for my next task: washing the dishes.

As I step toward the sink, I feel another wave of anger. Eddie Ryland insulted me again, and now I have to wash the fancy dishes that he just ate from. I take a few deep breaths, trying to calm down so that I don't accidentally break one of the delicate plates. Then I set to work.

It seems to take forever to wash—and dry—all the dishes that Elsa keeps carrying in from the dining room. When I'm finally finished, I'm so exhausted that I'm relieved to hear Elsa tell me it's time for bed.

Turn to page 66.

When we get back to Samantha's house, Grandmary hands the bottle of aspirin to Mrs. Hawkins. "With all due respect to Dr. Barnett's modern medicines," she says, "I prefer the tried-and-true willow-bark tea, don't you?"

Mrs. Hawkins nods. "I'll bring tea right away, ma'am," she says, "with a spoonful of cod-liver oil for good measure." Samantha wrinkles her nose in disgust, which prompts Mrs. Hawkins to promise *her* a spoonful, too.

Grandmary settles into a high-backed velvet chair and asks, "Does your mother have a telephone, dear? I can have Hawkins try to telephone your mother in the city."

I shake my head. Sure, my mom has a cell phone, but I'm pretty sure that Hawkins won't be able to reach her on that.

Grandmary says, "Well, it's decided then. You'll spend the night with us, and tomorrow we'll determine how best to return you safely to the city."

A sleepover at Samantha's? Samantha shoots me a grin, her brown eyes shining.

Grandmary spots someone in the hall beyond the

parlor. "Elsa, would you come here a moment?" she calls.

The sour-faced maid pokes her head into the room. "Yes, ma'am?" she asks shortly.

"Please set one more place for dinner," says Grandmary. "Our guest will be staying."

Elsa gives me a quick once-over and says, "Yes, ma'am." She turns and nearly bumps into Mrs. Hawkins, who is carrying a tray of tea with two teapots and several cups.

Before pouring the tea, Mrs. Hawkins takes a small brown bottle off the tray and pours me a spoonful of what must be cod-liver oil. The fishy smell greets me long before the spoon hits my lips.

"Hold your nose," Samantha urges, so I do. That helps with the taste, but the oily liquid running down my throat still makes me gag. I swallow hard and grimace, and then look on sympathetically as Samantha holds her own nose and reluctantly opens her mouth. After she's swallowed, too, she makes a face at me, which cracks me up.

As we drink our tea, though, I try to sit up straight and take small sips, just as Samantha does. It must take

forever to drink a whole cup this way.

"The Rylands will be here soon for dinner," Grandmary finally says, setting down her cup. "Samantha, perhaps you can find something in your wardrobe for your guest to wear?"

Turn to page 71.

Even though I'm tired, it's hard to fall asleep in my attic bedroom. I keep thinking of how Eddie has been treating me—as if I'm not good enough to be trusted just because I'm a servant. Even Elsa looked at me suspiciously when she asked if I had seen the brooch.

Then I think of Samantha. She doesn't seem to care whether I'm a servant or a celebrity. She just wants to be my friend. I say a quick thanks for her friendship.

When I finally fall asleep, I dream of being on trial in a courtroom. The crime I'm accused of? Stealing. And the prosecutor? Eddie Ryland, pacing the floor in his short little pants and bow tie. The judge starts banging a gavel against the bar: *rap, rap, rap . . .*

My eyes snap open in the sunlit tower room. I'm not in a courtroom—or at my dad's. Everything that happened yesterday comes rushing back to me.

I reach for the locket around my neck. Still there. Then I hear it again: *rap, rap, rap*. It's Samantha, poking her head into the room and knocking gently on the wall. "Are you awake, Ruby?" she whispers.

I'm relieved to see her, until I hear what she has to say. "Grandmary's new brooch is still missing, and

Elsa is pointing the finger at you."

I suddenly feel sick to my stomach. "Why is Elsa so mean to me?" I ask Samantha. "We're both servants here, but Elsa acts as if she's better than me. She keeps reminding me to keep 'my place.' And now she thinks I'm a thief?"

Samantha squares her shoulders and says, "Your place is right here, Ruby—right here with me. And you're no thief. I'm going to help you prove it. We just have to find the brooch."

Samantha says that she half suspects Elsa took the brooch herself. "I overheard her ask Grandmary for a raise in pay last week," she says, "and Grandmary said no. So maybe she took the brooch out of revenge—or because she needed the money for something."

Elsa? I hesitate. She's mean, all right, but that doesn't make her a thief.

To agree that Elsa might be guilty, turn to page 80.

To defend Elsa, turn to page 73.

I remember now what Samantha said about sharing a party line with neighbors. Does that mean they can listen in on one another's phone calls? Did Eddie hear every word of my conversation with the operator?

I stare at Eddie, wondering what to say or do. He looks so proud of himself. I fight the urge to put my hand on his face and push him right back into the bush he crawled out of.

"I'm telling," Eddie whispers with an annoying look that says he isn't bluffing.

Now what? I have to either tell Samantha what happened before Eddie does or find another way to get Eddie off my back. He looks as if he's gearing up to dart across the lawn and expose my secret right now.

To tell Samantha myself, turn to page 76.

To burst Eddie's bubble another way, turn to page 82.

As I follow Elsa toward the back door, Samantha waves at me from the kitchen table—and makes a face at Elsa's back. I smother a smile.

We're met by a balding man in a black suit on the porch, carrying a basket and a pair of clippers. Elsa introduces him as Hawkins, the butler. *The butler? Samantha and her grandmother must be very wealthy,* I think, wondering if there are any other servants I haven't yet met.

Elsa takes the basket and clippers from Hawkins and then shows me to the flower garden. "Fill this basket with fresh flowers for the dining room table," Elsa instructs. "Can you do that, girl?"

Elsa doesn't wait for a reply. She shakes her head and goes back into the kitchen.

I take one step into the garden and then freeze, not sure where to put my other foot. The garden is dense with flowers—I don't want to crush them. I wobble on one leg like a stork, and suddenly I hear giggling from behind me.

It's Samantha, stepping onto the porch. "Are you stuck in the flower garden?" she asks.

"I guess so," I say, grinning, as I try to hop back to the lawn beyond the flowers. I lose my balance and fall forward onto the grass.

Samantha laughs with me as she sits down on the lawn beside me. Then her face grows serious. She says softly, "Ruby, I'm sorry that you're on your own—that you lost your parents."

I flash back to that moment in the parlor when Samantha stood up for me because she thinks I'm an orphan. And now I feel guilty, because I'm not *really* an orphan—but Samantha is.

"I'm sorry about your parents, too," I say. Then we sit together quietly, side by side.

After a few moments, Samantha smiles and says, "Ruby, I have a feeling that you and I are going to be very good friends."

I have exactly the same feeling, I'm thinking when the porch door opens and I hear Elsa's now-familiar scolding. *"Ruby!"*

Turn to page 77.

I carefully set down my teacup and follow Samantha upstairs. "We'll find you something *perfect* to wear," she says. "It's a special treat to be able to eat with the adults."

A special treat? My mom insists that I eat dinner with her at the table most weeknights. A special treat at my house is being able to eat in front of the TV on movie night! But I'm excited to see what dinner is like at Samantha's house.

I pause on the plush floral rug just inside the bedroom door, taking it all in. Samantha's room is wall-papered with pink and white stripes. Delicate curtains frame a large window, and the head of Samantha's bed is draped with a high satin canopy trimmed with lace.

Samantha opens the doors of a large wooden cabinet. When I see what's inside, my jaw drops. Samantha has dresses in every color and fabric: plaid dresses with puffy sleeves, striped dresses with ruffled skirts, and satin dresses with lace collars. "Samantha, you're so lucky," I say, but she doesn't seem to hear. She's having too much fun picking out a dress for me.

"This one," she says, reaching for a lacy lilac-colored dress with a lavender satin bow at the waist.

I pull off my capris and am about to step into the dress when Samantha holds up her hand. "Wait! You forgot your undergarments. Here's a chemise," she says, pulling a long, frilly undershirt out of the cabinet, "and a pair of drawers."

Drawers? When I pull on the lace-trimmed undergarment, it stretches down to my knees. I look up at Samantha, stifling a giggle. She's already handing me the next piece of clothing: a lacy skirt she calls a petticoat.

By the time I go downstairs, I'm also wearing long stockings with straps, or "garters," to hold them up, and high-buttoned boots. I've got a huge lavender bow in my hair, and when I step through the doorway, I fight the urge to duck. But my dress *swishes* as I walk, and I have to admit—I feel like a wealthy young lady. My silver heart-shaped locket, now hanging around my neck, is the finishing touch.

Turn to page 78.

I don't know," I say to Samantha. "We don't have any proof that she's a thief. Could something else have happened?"

Samantha takes a deep breath. "Let's think," she says, staring at the ceiling. "Wait, I know! You did the wash yesterday. Maybe the brooch was on Grand-mary's dress and fell off into a washtub. Or it could be in the grass under the clothesline!"

Samantha's eagerness to hunt down the brooch—and prove my innocence—gets my own heart racing. I leap to my feet, tempted to run outside right now.

"Wait!" says Samantha, reaching for my hand. "Elsa is expecting you downstairs. Go down and act as if everything is normal. We'll search the lawn the first chance we get later today."

I nod and smile at Samantha. "Good plan." Then I dress and wash up quickly.

Sure enough, Elsa is waiting for me in the kitchen with breakfast and my first task for the morning: ironing. "You'll heat the irons on the stovetop," she says, reaching for some matches in a metal holder above the stove.

There's a loud knock on the back door. Elsa scowls.

"It's the milkman," she says. "He always comes at the most inconvenient times." She hands me the matches and tells me to light the stove.

Me? My parents never let me use matches at home, and since when does a stove need to be lit anyway? I turn to Mrs. Hawkins for help, but she's on the telephone ordering meat from a butcher.

When Elsa comes back in, I'm still holding the matches. She takes them from me in disgust and lights the burners herself. She sets three heavy irons on the stove and says, "You'll rotate the irons, see now? You'll use one or two while the other is heating on the stove, so when you bring a cool one inside, there'll be a hot one waiting for you. Understand?"

I nod, wondering just how hot those irons are going to get—and how I'm going to carry them without burning myself.

I'm relieved when Elsa helps me carry the hot irons outside. I'm eager to search the grass for the brooch, but Elsa is keeping a close eye on me today—maybe to make sure I don't "steal" anything else.

After lunch, Samantha and I finally get our chance to search the grass. I'm hanging clothes *again* (to "air

them out") when Samantha comes outside saying the coast is clear.

We start with the washtub full of clean clothes at my feet. "Let's stack them on the grass," Samantha says, "and tip the tub on its side."

After we empty the tub, I inspect it. I run my hands along the bottom, hoping to feel the brooch. There's nothing there.

I'm about to tell Samantha that there's another tub inside when Elsa storms out the back door and scolds me for putting fresh laundry in the grass. "What is the matter with you, girl?" she asks. "Dirtying clean laundry and socializing with Miss Samantha? You need to remember your place."

There it is again: *Remember your place.*

Samantha hears it, too, and I see the look in her eye—a look that I now know means *I'm not giving up.*

Turn to page 87.

ou don't have to tell," I say to Eddie. "I'm going to tell Samantha myself."

Eddie sneers at me. "I bet you won't," he says.

"I bet I *will*," I say, annoyed that I'm letting Eddie get under my skin. "Watch me."

I whirl around and march over to Samantha, who is sitting on the porch steps.

"What does pesky Eddie want?" Samantha asks, shooting Eddie a look. He locks eyes with her for a few seconds and then seems to lose his nerve. He pulls his head back through the hedge and disappears.

I square my shoulders and turn to face Samantha myself. She has been so incredibly nice to me. I have to tell her the truth about the phone call before she hears it from someone else—especially someone like Eddie.

"Samantha," I say, "here's the thing . . ."

Turn to page 89.

Samantha's face flushes at the sound of Elsa's voice. "I'm sorry," she whispers. "I'll see you tonight." She hurries up the porch steps and brushes past Elsa. The grumpy maid looks as if she's about to reprimand Samantha, but she has bigger fish to fry with me.

"Ruby," she says again, "a body has enough to do without looking after you. Have you clipped a single blossom?" She glances dramatically into my empty basket. "No, you have not. Yet you've managed to find time to socialize. You're a servant—*not* a friend to Miss Samantha. You need to keep your place. Do you understand?"

Elsa's words feel like a punch to the stomach: *You're a servant—not a friend.* She says it as if it's a fact, as if everyone should know that a rich girl like Samantha and a servant girl like me can't be friends.

But Samantha and I *are* friends. I can feel it when I'm with her. And as long as there's a chance I can spend more time with her, I'll stick around—no matter what Elsa thinks or says.

Turn to page 84.

Hawkins leads us into the dining room, where everyone is dressed elegantly. Grandmary sits at one end of the table like a queen on her throne, and at the opposite end is a man in a suit coat who must be Mr. Ryland. Beside him sits Mrs. Ryland, a red-headed woman in a rose-colored gown who gives me such a haughty look that I'm tempted to hide behind Samantha. Then I see the freckle-faced boy seated beside her: it's Eddie, the boy from the lilac bushes! He's staring at me as if I have two heads.

Avoiding Eddie's gaze, I glance down at the fancy place setting in front of me. A pretty china plate rests on the crisp white tablecloth, surrounded by an array of gleaming silver: three forks on the left and two spoons and a knife on the right. My water glass looks like a crystal goblet, and my napkin is folded into a long tubular shape. Elsa may be a grumpy maid, but she sure knows how to set a table. I'm afraid to touch anything.

Just then Elsa pushes through the swinging door with a tray of steaming bowls. I catch sight of Mrs. Hawkins in the kitchen behind her, bustling around with red cheeks and a towel thrown over one

shoulder. I realize then that there's no place setting at this table for her or for Elsa. Samantha's servants are working hard to prepare dinner for us, but *they* won't be enjoying it anytime soon.

As Elsa sets a bowl of soup before me, the salty smell wafts upward, and my mouth starts to water. I didn't realize how hungry I was until this very moment. I can barely wait the few seconds it'll take to lift a spoonful to my lips. But which spoon do I use?

To pick up a spoon and start eating, turn to page 85.

To wait to see which spoon Samantha chooses, turn to page 99.

ou might be right," I say to Samantha. "But how do we prove it?"

"There's only one way," Samantha says. "We have to catch Elsa with the brooch. We should search her room—right now."

"Now?" I say.

Samantha nods urgently. "I just saw her setting the breakfast table," she explains. "This is our best chance."

I follow Samantha down the creaky stairs to the next floor. Elsa's door is shut, but Samantha reaches boldly for the doorknob.

What will happen if we get caught? Samantha's risking her own hide to help me. Will she get into trouble, too?

I follow Samantha into Elsa's room and quickly shut the door. When I turn around, I'm surprised to see how bare it is. The narrow bed is made up with a simple bedspread. There's a wooden nightstand beside the bed, but it's empty except for a grainy black-and-white photograph of a large family.

Samantha tiptoes toward a tall wooden wardrobe and eases open the door. A shawl and two plain dresses are hanging from the bar. Samantha reaches

up to the top shelf of the wardrobe and pulls down a large round hatbox. She sets the box on the bed and lifts the lid, revealing a straw hat. No surprise there.

"I don't see the brooch," I whisper.

"Wait," Samantha says, removing the hat. There, in the bottom of the hatbox, is a thick, banded stack of dollar bills!

Turn to page 97.

Don't worry about it, Eddie," I say. "I'm not going to Piney Point."

His face darkens. "Well, you're still a liar," he says before disappearing back into the hedge.

I *do* feel like a liar. If there were a way to ask my dad for permission to go to Piney Point, I would do it. But there isn't, and besides, he would probably say no. He's strict about how I spend my time when I'm with him. I flash back to the rules my dad laid out about the Internet: no e-mailing, blogging, or posting online without his permission. "The Internet is a very public place," he'd said. *Apparently phone lines a hundred years ago were, too,* I think to myself.

I suddenly feel an ache of homesickness. I miss my dad, kind of the way I did when my parents first got divorced. Funny how that feeling comes and goes—and then comes back again, just when I think I'm getting over it.

I need to tell Samantha that I can't go with her to Piney Point. If I don't, Eddie will. And besides, I'm ready now to go home and see my dad.

I invite Samantha to sit with me beneath the oak tree. "Samantha," I say sadly, "I can't go to Piney Point

with you. The truth is, I miss my family. I think I should catch the first train to Plattsburgh tomorrow."

Samantha looks away, but she says sweetly, "It's all right. I know what it's like to miss your family."

As Samantha heads inside to track down Grandmary again, I lean against the tree, wishing I knew how to cheer her up. When I put my hands in my pockets, I discover the friendship bracelet Stella made for me. *What else have I been carrying around in my capris?* I wonder, patting my pockets.

"Bloomers," Samantha called them when I first met her. That was when she told me that she'd never ridden a bike.

As I tie Stella's friendship bracelet around my wrist, I suddenly have an idea—the perfect way to thank Samantha for being a friend to me.

To give her a lesson in bike riding, turn to page 94.

To offer her the friendship bracelet, turn to page 103.

Elsa has one more task for me: cleaning out the fireplace in the parlor. "I've already brushed the carpets," Elsa explains, "so mind that you dump the ash in the scuttle and not on the floor." I nod, wondering what on earth a "scuttle" is.

She hands me a metal container that looks like a gravy boat. I use a small shovel and broom to carefully sweep the ashes from the fireplace into the scuttle.

When the fireplace is clean, I stand up to stretch. On the mantel, I see a beautiful black lace fan resting against the mirror, half open.

I pick up the fan and open it fully, admiring its shimmering pearl handle. As I hold the fan to my face and gaze into the mirror, I don't feel like a servant girl anymore. I feel like the lady of the house.

"Pleased to meet you, I'm sure," I say, fanning my face and dropping into a low curtsy.

Hearing footsteps in the hall, I snap the fan shut, drop it onto the mantel, and whirl around. My long stiff dress swings against the scuttle and knocks it over. A pile of gray ash spills out onto the carpet.

Turn to page 91.

I choose the largest spoon and scoop up a hot mouthful of soup. As I take a slow slurp, careful not to spill on my fancy dress, I catch Samantha's expression out of the corner of my eye. She looks horrified. Only then do I realize that she—and everyone else at the table—is sitting still, with their hands in their laps, waiting. Waiting for what?

Then Grandmary lifts her spoon, and at that moment, the others at the table reach for their spoons, too. A hot flush creeps across my cheeks. Samantha glances nervously from me to Grandmary, and I know I've done something horribly wrong.

There are a lot of rules at a fancy dinner in 1904. This isn't anything like eating at the kitchen table with Mom!

Eddie says in a loud whisper, "What a ninny. Don't you have any manners?"

"Eddie!" Mrs. Ryland scolds. "Mind your own manners—and don't talk with your mouth full." Then she turns to me and asks, "So, dear, what does your father do in the city?"

I put my spoon down and answer as politely as I can. "Actually, ma'am, my father doesn't live in the city.

My mom has a job there, though, as a social worker."

Samantha glances up, startled. "Your mother *works*?" She looks impressed.

Don't most moms work? But then I see Mrs. Ryland raise an eyebrow and purse her lips. Apparently not.

Turn to page 105.

As soon as Elsa steps back inside, Samantha drops to her knees in the grass, and I quickly join her. We sweep the grass, side to side, with open fingers. I feel like the luckiest girl in the world when I spot that brooch twinkling beneath the clothesline. It's shaped like a dragonfly, with ruby eyes and turquoise wings.

"That's it!" Samantha shrieks as my fingers close around the brooch. She jumps to her feet and brushes off her pinafore. "Let's take it to Grandmary right away," she says.

We race through the kitchen, run past Elsa—whose mouth is hanging open—and nearly knock over Mrs. Hawkins in the hallway. "Where's Grandmary?" Samantha asks breathlessly.

"Good heavens, love," says Mrs. Hawkins. "Slow down! Your grandmother is having tea in the parlor with Mrs. Ryland."

Samantha races ahead of me down the hall and then takes a moment to compose herself just outside the parlor door. When we step inside, Mrs. Edwards and Mrs. Ryland, a woman with red hair like her son's, glance up in surprise.

"Show her, Ruby," Samantha urges me, and I proudly stretch out my hand to present the dragonfly brooch to Mrs. Edwards.

"Oh, well done, girls!" she says. "Wherever did you find it?"

"In the grass outside!" says Samantha excitedly. But I notice that Mrs. Ryland is eyeing me suspiciously, as if I just pulled the brooch out of my sleeve.

"The grass?" Mrs. Ryland says. "What an unlikely place." She sniffs and takes a long sip of tea.

Samantha juts out her chin and says exactly what I wish I could. "It was a *very* likely place, actually," she says. "The brooch fell off while Ruby was doing the wash."

"Samantha," Mrs. Edwards scolds. "Please mind your tone." She dismisses us, but the warmth in her blue-gray eyes tells me that she doesn't suspect me of stealing. So why does Mrs. Ryland?

Turn to page 104.

I tell Samantha about how I wasn't able to reach my family by telephone, but how I pretended to be talking with them anyway. "I really wanted to go with you to Piney Point," I say. "I guess I'm not ready to be with my family yet."

I expect Samantha to be angry with me, but instead, she looks curious. "Why aren't you ready to be with your family?" she asks.

It's a tough question, but I try to answer it honestly. "I don't know them very well," I say. "And I miss my mom so much. I wish I could be with her this summer just as I've always been, but I can't."

Those words strike a chord with Samantha. She wraps her arm around my shoulder and leans in. "*That* part I understand," she says kindly.

I remember then what she told me about her parents when I first met her. "Samantha," I ask hesitantly, "do you miss your mom, too?"

She stares at some faraway place and nods. Then she asks in a small voice, "Does that sound silly, to miss someone you don't remember very well?"

I shake my head. Sometimes I forget what it was like to have my parents together, but I miss it all the

same. "No," I say firmly. "I don't think that's silly at all."

Samantha smiles and then straightens up, as if she's suddenly had an idea. "Is your family expecting you today?" she asks. "Will they be worried if you arrive a few days late?"

I can answer that truthfully, because I know my locket will take me "home," where time seems to stand still. "They won't worry," I assure Samantha. "They aren't expecting me yet."

The gleam in Samantha's eyes suggests that I've given her the answer she was hoping for. "Then I think you should come with me to Piney Point," she declares. "And maybe after some time there, you'll feel better about going to see your family."

Relief washes over me. I've confessed the truth to Samantha, and she's not angry. And the day after tomorrow, we'll leave for Piney Point!

Turn to page 109.

Elsa and Grandmary reach the parlor at the same time, responding to my shriek. When they see the soiled carpet, I wait for the scolding, but it doesn't come. Instead, a fuming Elsa apologizes to Grandmary and says she'll clean up the mess right away.

"No, let me clean it up," I offer quickly. "Please, just show me where you keep the vacuum."

Elsa scoffs and says, "Vacuums? Do you know nothing, girl? No one uses such ridiculous contraptions as those modern machines in homes like this. We'd need a horse just to pull one. No, we'll use the carpet sweeper. *I'll* use the carpet sweeper," she corrects herself, taking me by the arm and hurrying me out of the room.

As I pass Grandmary, I see the worry in her face: for me, or for the soiled rug in the parlor? Either way, I feel terrible. I didn't mean to cause trouble for her, this woman who was willing to take a chance on me. I even feel a little sorry for Elsa, who has to clean that rug again—without a vacuum cleaner.

Elsa is silent during the long, painful walk up to my tower room. When we finally get there, I stand still,

nervously twisting the hem of my apron, while Elsa paces.

"Mrs. Edwards's guests will arrive soon for dinner," Elsa says, speaking slowly and firmly, "and the best place for *you* is right here. You're not to leave this room. Do you understand?"

I can't meet Elsa's eyes, but I nod.

When Elsa leaves, I wrap my arms around my chest, holding back tears. Is it time to go home now? I feel as if I've made a huge mess here, but I know I can't leave without saying good-bye to Samantha.

My stomach growls, breaking the silence of the room. Will Elsa bring me dinner? Or will she make me go without to teach me a lesson?

I picture the guests sitting around the fancy dinner table downstairs. Is the table the picture of perfection, just as Elsa hoped it would be? I imagine the bouquet of fresh flowers in the middle of the table, and the elegant settings and folded napkins. I can almost smell the delicious foods coming from Mrs. Hawkins's kitchen—until my stomach rumbles again, telling me that it's time to think about something else.

An hour passes, maybe two. I tiptoe down the stairs

to the third floor and press my ear to the door, listening for sounds of Elsa in the hallway or in her room. Surely dinner is over by now. My insides feel so empty that it hurts. Should I sneak down to the kitchen to try to find something to eat?

To tiptoe downstairs,
turn to page 101.

To stay put,
turn to page 107.

After a quick chat with Hawkins, who agrees to help me with a thank-you surprise for Samantha, I head inside for dinner. I barely taste the food that Mrs. Hawkins sets in front of me. I'm too excited about my plans for after dinner. When Grandmary retires to the parlor, I grab Samantha's hand and invite her outside.

"But why?" she asks, tripping along the porch steps behind me.

"Just follow me," I say secretively.

So she does, all the way across the yard to what Hawkins calls the "carriage house." I knock on the door of the shed, and a moment later Hawkins walks out, wheeling a bicycle. When Samantha sees it, her eyes grow wide.

"Can I teach you how to ride before I go?" I ask.

Samantha's cheeks flush pink. Nervously she glances at the house, as if waiting for Grandmary to appear and put the kibosh on all of this. But then she nods eagerly and steps toward the bike. Hawkins and I help her climb on, and she tucks her skirts beneath her legs so that they won't get stuck in the bike chain.

Hawkins runs beside Samantha across the yard,

letting go when she seems to have enough speed and balance to ride on her own. She wobbles, steadies herself, and then . . . crashes sideways into the grass.

Samantha isn't hurt, but she's discouraged. Her dress is stuck in the bicycle chain, and Hawkins has to pull the chain backward to release the torn, grease-streaked hem.

Samantha looks defeated, but now I'm more determined than ever to teach her how to ride. "It's your dress," I say. "You need bloomers. Why don't you try mine?"

A few minutes later, Samantha steps out of the shed wearing my capris, and I follow behind wearing her dress and pinafore. We're both giggling—she at the freedom of her new pants, and me at the thought of ever hopping on a bike wearing what I'm wearing now. No wonder girls in Samantha's time didn't ride bikes. With so many long layers, I'd crash for sure!

In her bloomers, Samantha climbs onto the bicycle with a new kind of confidence. She makes a successful ride across the yard, and Hawkins is there to help her turn around and start back across. There's a huge smile on her face, and I'm not sure if it's from the

thrill of riding a bike for the first time or the freedom of wearing pants. She's picking up speed when the back door of the house creaks open.

"Sa*man*tha!" Grandmary's voice booms across the yard.

Turn to page 121.

"It's proof!" Samantha whispers triumphantly. "How else could she have gotten all of this money? Elsa must have stolen Grandmary's brooch and sold it! We have to tell Grandmary right away."

Samantha tucks the money back into the hatbox and quietly puts it back in the wardrobe. Then we rush downstairs.

Mrs. Hawkins stops us in the hall just outside the parlor. "Time for breakfast, Miss Samantha," she says. "Your grandmother is waiting for you in the dining room."

Samantha gives me a look that says *I've got this,* and then hurries toward the dining room.

Mrs. Hawkins waves me into the kitchen. "I have muffins waiting for you, too, child," she says. I can smell them as soon as I step into the room. I eat slowly, straining my ears to try to hear the voices from the dining room.

When Elsa steps into the kitchen, I nearly drop my muffin. "There you are, Ruby," she says. "Daylight's a-wasting, and we have a great deal to do today. Finish up your breakfast, and I'll get you started on the ironing."

But then Grandmary calls out from the dining room, "Elsa? I need to see you right away."

Elsa's face darkens. She casts a questioning glance at Mrs. Hawkins, who gives the slightest shrug. Then Elsa disappears through the swinging door.

Turn to page 111.

Samantha isn't eating yet. She's staring at Grandmary, who carefully lays her napkin in her lap and then reaches for her spoon. As she lifts the spoon, I see the others at the table reach for their own. That's my cue: I choose the largest spoon before me and dip it into my soup.

As we eat, I try to follow Samantha's lead, afraid that there might be other dinnertime "rules" that I don't know about. I take small sips of soup and listen as Mrs. Ryland tells Grandmary about a recent trip she took to the city.

"We steered clear of Madison Square Park, of course," says Mrs. Ryland. "Those suffragists were making a spectacle of themselves, hoisting signs and carrying on."

Suffragists? I'm wondering what the word means—and how to ask politely. I fight the urge to raise my hand, as if I were in school. Instead, I wipe my mouth and ask, "Excuse me, Mrs. Ryland, but what's a suffragist?"

"A *suffragist,*" Mrs. Ryland says, emphasizing the word as if it's dirty, "is a person who believes that women should have the right to vote in political

elections, as men do. What utter nonsense." She makes a *tsk-tsk* sound and reaches for her glass of water.

I flash back to the last election. My mother didn't just vote—she plastered her car with bumper stickers and carried signs supporting our favorite candidate. Sometimes it was embarrassing, but when our candidate won, I was proud of my mom. I felt as if she had made a difference.

What if someone had told my mom she couldn't vote in that election? What if I would never be able to help decide who would hold some of the most important jobs in the country?

Turn to page 112.

After cracking open the door to make sure the coast is clear, I tiptoe down the hallway and inch my way past Elsa's room, willing the floorboards not to creak. The door is closed and a light is on—she must be inside.

I make my way down the next staircase and stop on the landing, listening for sounds from Samantha's bedroom. Nothing.

As I tiptoe down the last staircase, I hear the clatter of dishes in the kitchen. The lingering scent of cinnamon and apples reaches my nose, and I can almost taste the tart that Grandmary's guests had for dessert. Through a crack in the door, I see Mrs. Hawkins standing beside the sink. On the table between us, a loaf of sliced bread rests in a basket. My stomach twists at the sight of it. Plain bread has never looked so delicious.

When Grandmary calls to Mrs. Hawkins from down the hall, she dries her hands on a dish towel and hurries out of the kitchen. It's now or never. I dart toward the bread.

My fingers close around a couple of thick slices. I take a big bite, savoring the taste for just a moment,

and then tiptoe back toward the stairs.

Before I can make my way back up, though, I hear the quick steps of someone coming down. I stand there, frozen, watching the long skirts rounding the stairs above.

Elsa.

Turn to page 116.

I find Samantha in the kitchen, and I take her hand and lead her to the parlor. "Before I go," I say to her, "I want to give you something." I untie the friendship bracelet from my wrist and reach over to tie it onto Samantha's.

"A very good friend of mine made this for me," I say. "And while I've been here, you've been a good friend, too. Will you wear this and remember me?"

Samantha stares at the bracelet and then looks up at me, her eyes shining. She nods and leans over to give me a hug. When she pulls away, she says, "I wish there was something I could give you."

I shake my head. "You've done a lot for me already, Samantha," I say. "You helped me through a pretty bumpy time." I rub my forehead, and Samantha giggles.

Turn to page 115.

"I don't understand," I say to Samantha after we've gone back outside. "Why does Mrs. Ryland dislike me? She doesn't even know me."

Samantha shrugs sadly. "Mrs. Ryland doesn't treat you well because you're a servant," she explains. "It's not right, but that's how a lot of people are, I'm afraid."

"But it's so unfair!" I say, my voice rising.

"I know," Samantha says. "I'm sorry, Ruby."

I take a deep, calming breath. It's not Samantha's fault that things are this way. "It's funny," I tell her, "because you—the girl I'm supposed to be working for—treat me better than anyone. Thank you for everything you've done for me, Samantha. I'll always remember it."

Her face falls. "You say that as if you'll be leaving soon," she says softly.

Turn to page 114.

social worker?" Mrs. Ryland repeats in a high-pitched tone. "What does your mother do, specifically?"

I'm embarrassed to realize that I don't really know much about my mom's job. I put down my spoon and take a sip of water from the heavy crystal goblet in front of me. "She . . . um . . . helps homeless families, or children whose parents can't take care of them," I finally say.

Samantha stares at me. "Jiminy," she says, "it sounds as if your mom helps people who really need it." Then she says to Mrs. Ryland, "We met a woman today who is training to be a *doctor.* She's lucky to do such important work. She was helping a boy with chicken pox—"

"Samantha," Grandmary says quickly. "A doctor's visit is hardly suitable dinner conversation. Please remember your manners."

Samantha's face falls, and she sits back in her chair. At the words *chicken pox,* I sit back, too, scratching my suddenly itchy back against the wooden chair.

"Lucky to do such work?" says Mrs. Ryland. "I hardly think there's any good fortune in a woman

needing to work outside the home, especially in such a—well, *unsanitary* profession. Mary, don't you agree?"

Grandmary takes that opportunity to ring a dinner bell and ask Elsa to bring more bread.

Turn to page 112.

Elsa was very clear about me not leaving this room, so despite my hunger pangs, I don't. I'm sitting cross-legged on the blanket, counting the boards in the ceiling, when I hear footsteps on the stairs.

It's Samantha, bringing dinner for me in a tin pail. "It's not much," she says, pulling out bread, cheese, an apple, and a gingerbread cookie. "But Mrs. Hawkins knew you must be hungry."

I thank her and take a juicy bite of apple.

Samantha waits until I've finished my apple, and then she blurts, "I think they're going to send you away, Ruby. I heard that nasty Elsa complaining to Grandmary, trying to make trouble for you."

I sigh and drop my hands to my lap. "I'm not surprised Elsa wants to send me away, Samantha," I say. "I *did* make more work for her—and there was plenty for her to do already in a big house like this."

Samantha looks amazed to hear me defending Elsa. "You're a good person, Ruby," she says. "But if Grandmary sends you away, where will you go? Not to an orphanage, I hope!" Her eyes are wide.

"No," I say quickly. I may be going home to a long, lonely summer at my dad's house, but not to an

orphanage. "Whatever happens," I add, "I'm really glad I met you."

Samantha looks away. "Me, too," she says in a wobbly voice, "but I was so hoping we would become friends."

"We *have* become friends," I assure her. "You stood up for me. You made my chores a lot more fun, and even now—well, look, you brought me dinner, and you're worried about where I'm going next. Samantha, you've been a really, really good friend."

Samantha smiles, her cheeks pink. "You have, too, Ruby," she says warmly. She straightens up and says, "I should let you rest now. Maybe things will seem better in the morning. Let's both hope for that, all right?"

I smile and nod. And as Samantha starts down the stairs, I can't help feeling a little bit better—and less scared about tomorrow.

Turn to page 125.

The next morning, Grandmary asks Samantha and me to stay "out from underfoot" so that Elsa and Mrs. Hawkins can finish preparations for Piney Point. "Do you need to pack a suitcase?" I ask Samantha.

"Oh, no," she says. "Elsa will take care of that."

"Really?" I say, but then I realize I haven't seen Samantha do any chores since I've been here. She has a servant to do everything from making her bed to packing her suitcase.

Must be nice, I think, but then I wonder what it would feel like to have someone else packing my clothes and deciding what I'm going to wear.

A moment later, I know *just* how it feels. Grandmary isn't going to let me wear my "bloomers" on the train to Piney Point. She asks Samantha to take me to meet their seamstress, Jessie, who is altering one of Samantha's play dresses to fit me.

Samantha leads me up two staircases and down a long hall to the sewing room. There I meet Jessie, a kind, pretty black woman. "Ah, here you are, miss," she says, standing to hold up a red-checked dress in front of me. She smooths the fabric and says, "If we

lengthen this a tad, I think it will work quite nicely."

Jessie helps me try on the dress so that she can measure the length. As I step into the dress and turn in circles before Jessie, Samantha watches me, a smile playing at the corners of her lips. I'll bet she wishes she were trying on *my* clothing instead. Something tells me Samantha would wear bloomers every day if she could.

After trying on this heavy dress—with an apron-like pinafore on top and three layers of undergarments underneath—I kind of agree with Samantha. It's a warm summer day outside, and I'm already starting to sweat.

Turn to page 117.

A few minutes later, Grandmary comes into the kitchen. She motions for Mrs. Hawkins to join her in the butler's pantry, and then Samantha comes into the kitchen and waves me toward the back door.

"Elsa is leaving," Samantha says as soon as we're outside. "Grandmary asked her about the money in the hatbox, and Elsa got very upset. I don't know if she took the brooch, but she sure looked guilty."

Samantha and I are standing near the lilac tunnel when we hear a horse-drawn carriage pull up in front of the house. Elsa has packed up really quickly, which I guess is no surprise given how few possessions she has. And then—just like that—Elsa is gone.

As we walk back toward the house, I kick something with the toe of my shoe. It lands a few feet ahead of me and sparkles in the morning sunlight. Samantha sees it, too, and we both stop walking.

When Samantha reaches for the object, the color drains from her face. I know what she's holding before she even shows it to me: *Grandmary's brooch.*

Turn to page 180.

Samantha breaks the silence that follows. "My uncle Gard's friend Cornelia says that women should have all the same opportunities as men," she says, looking at me but talking loudly enough for the others to hear. "She thinks women should be able to vote in elections and earn their own money so that they don't have to depend on men for everything."

Mrs. Ryland stares at Samantha, mouth open. "Is that right?" she says, her voice rising again. "Is that what Cornelia says? Well, in my opinion—"

"Cornelia says a great many things," Grandmary interjects, "none of which should be your concern, Samantha. Now let's focus more on your food and less on Cornelia's newfangled notions." She gives Samantha a steady, steely gaze that says, *This conversation is finished.*

"Yes, ma'am," Samantha says softly, staring at the baked chicken and string beans that Elsa has just placed before her.

But Mrs. Ryland is all fired up now. "Really, Mary," she says, "I had no idea you were raising a young suffragist under your very own roof."

As Mrs. Ryland speaks, Mr. Ryland reaches for

another piece of bread. With each word that comes out of her mouth, he puts another bite of food into his own. Something tells me that he barely gets a word in edgewise in the Ryland household.

It's Eddie who saves the day—by flinging a bean across the table at Samantha and giving his mother a place to direct her outrage. She scolds him fiercely throughout the main course.

The food keeps coming: a green salad, and then a dessert plate of fruit, nuts, and fancy little tarts. I'm amazed at how much Mrs. Hawkins made in that old-fashioned kitchen without the help of a microwave.

As I take a not-so-dainty bite of the tart, a chunk of crust falls into my lap. I glance at Samantha, wondering if she noticed, but she's staring at her own lap, playing with the edges of her napkin. She hasn't said a word since Grandmary scolded her, and her tart rests on her dessert plate, untouched.

Turn to page 143.

I realize then that Samantha's right—the time has come for me to go. I'll miss her, but I don't think I can pretend to be Ruby for even one more night, not when Elsa keeps reminding me to "keep my place" and people like Mrs. Ryland treat me like a thief or a second-class person.

"I do have to go," I say softly.

Samantha nods sadly. "But what if you're treated unfairly in your next job, too?" she asks. "Or they work you even harder than Elsa did here?"

I think about the "work" I'll have to do at my dad's house, picturing again the chore chart on the refrigerator. *No problem,* I think to myself. After what I went through yesterday and today, any chore in my dad's house seems like a piece of cake.

"I'll be treated fairly," I assure Samantha. "I'll make sure of it. My family will make sure of it."

Samantha looks relieved. When we hear Mrs. Edwards calling, she gives me a quick hug and hurries inside.

Turn to page 120.

The next morning, I'm on the train, which is pulling slowly away from the station. When I can no longer see Samantha and Hawkins waving to me from the platform, I start to think about home. I was so lonely without Stella at first, but making a friend in Samantha helped fill that hole in my heart. Now I'm going to go back to my dad's missing Samantha, too. What will make *that* feel better?

I picture Gracie's face. She's so excited about having a new sister. I wish I felt the same way, but my mom says that it might take time. Gracie and I can't become sisters overnight. *But,* I wonder, *could we start by being friends?*

As I reach for my locket, I imagine Gracie's face when I walk through the bedroom door and ask her if she'd like to do a project with me. Then I picture the box of craft supplies that I brought from home. There's embroidery floss in the box—the kind used to make friendship bracelets. I'll make one for Gracie, and then maybe I'll teach her how to make one for me.

The End

To read this story another way and see how different choices lead to a different ending, turn back to page 17.

I step backward into the kitchen, but it's too late. Elsa follows me and demands an explanation, but I can't speak. The bread is stuck in my throat. I can't swallow it down, and I for sure can't spit it out. I can only stand there, looking guilty as charged, as Elsa begins her rant. Mrs. Hawkins hurries back into the kitchen looking very confused.

After Elsa lectures me about stealing food and disobeying orders, she pushes past me and grabs a teakettle from the stove. She starts filling the kettle with water from the sink, as if to wash her hands of me.

Mrs. Hawkins catches me just before I start back up the stairs. "Servants eat after the others," she whispers. "I would have sent you some food. But now . . ." She raises her hands helplessly at her sides.

Over Mrs. Hawkins's shoulder, I see Samantha's pale face appear in the hallway beyond the kitchen. She starts toward me, but Mrs. Hawkins stops her with a gentle shake of her head. Sadly, I begin my long ascent back to the tower room.

Turn to page 122.

The next morning, I'm wearing the red-checked dress and riding in a horse-drawn carriage to the Mount Bedford train station. As I board the train to Piney Point, I'm grateful for my borrowed clothing. The other passengers are dressed as elegantly as Grandmary in her tailored jacket and skirt. And the train car itself is fancy, too, with ornately carved woodwork, velvet curtains, and two rows of plush chairs.

As Samantha and I take seats just behind Grandmary, I notice that Elsa and Mr. and Mrs. Hawkins are no longer with us. "Servants ride in a separate coach car," Samantha explains.

I'm not sure what a "coach car" is, but I have a feeling it's not as beautiful or as comfortable as this one. That makes me feel sad for the Hawkinses—and even for grumpy Elsa. What did I do to deserve this car? And why should they, who worked so hard to prepare for Piney Point, have to ride somewhere else?

During the daylong trip to Piney Point, we switch trains several times. As we board our last train, I squirm in my seat, trying to adjust the long underwear I'm wearing beneath my dress. Grandmary insisted I wear it so that I wouldn't "catch cold" on the trip.

In June? I wonder as I reach down to scratch my leg.

Samantha notices and gives me an apologetic shrug. "I have to wear long underwear from September until the end of June," she admits. "Grandmary's rules."

I'm actually grateful for the long underwear, though, when we settle onto a steamboat to cross Goose Lake, our last leg of the trip. A damp fog hangs over the water, and there's a chilly breeze.

As we approach the shoreline of Piney Point, the steamboat blasts its whistle, and Samantha strains her eyes to see Uncle Gard, who should be waiting for us on the dock. "There he is!" she shouts excitedly.

At the sight of us, Uncle Gard breaks into some sort of jig, which makes me giggle. I have a feeling I'm going to like Uncle Gard.

The steam engine of the boat hisses softly as we come to rest beside the wooden dock. The next thing I know, Hawkins is helping me off the boat. "Easy does it, miss," he says kindly, not letting go until I find my footing.

"Hello, Sam!" Uncle Gard calls as he swoops Samantha into his arms. He's handsome, with dark hair and a mustache. When she introduces him to me,

he makes a dramatic bow and kisses my hand, which makes my cheeks flush hot.

There's an older man with white hair and twinkly blue eyes standing on the dock behind Uncle Gard. Samantha gives him a warm hug, too, and introduces him to me as Admiral Beemis, Grandmary's friend from England. He's a retired ship captain who visits Piney Point every summer.

Then I see a pretty ginger-haired woman on shore, waving at us and shielding her eyes from the sun. "Hello, Miss Cornelia!" Samantha calls to her. "That's Uncle Gard's friend. It's her first time here, too," she whispers in my ear as we step off the dock and onto solid ground.

Turn to page 123.

A few minutes later, I hear Mrs. Edwards calling me inside, too. I follow her into the parlor.

"Ruby," Mrs. Edwards says, "I'd like to apologize for all of the upset surrounding my missing brooch. I hope you know that I consider you a trustworthy girl. Samantha tells me, however, that you have chosen not to continue on with us. Is that so?"

"Yes, Mrs. Edwards," I say. "I appreciate the work you've given me, but it's time for me to go home."

I'm surprised to see the disappointment in Mrs. Edwards's eyes. "Very well. Let's settle up, then. You haven't been here a full week, but I think you've earned this." She pulls out an envelope from her desk, and from that envelope, a crisp dollar bill. As she hands it to me, the work I've done during the last two days flashes through my mind.

I sure didn't earn much money, but I did learn a lot. I learned how—and how not—to treat people. And I learned what real work is. When I get home, I'll offer to do more chores—anything *except* the laundry.

The End

To read this story another way and see how different choices lead to a different ending, turn back to page 15.

Samantha skids to an unladylike stop. When she untangles her legs from the bike and brushes herself off, she gives Grandmary a quick curtsy.

"What on earth are you doing?" Grandmary asks.

The look on Samantha's face—so different from how she looked just moments ago—makes me so sad, I have to do something.

"It was my idea, ma'am," I say, mustering all my courage. "You and Samantha have been so nice to me. I wanted to give Samantha a gift in return, and I know how much she wanted to learn how to ride a bicycle. Please don't be angry with Samantha."

I feel Samantha's hand reach for mine and give my fingers a grateful squeeze.

Hawkins takes a step forward, too. "Madam," he says, as dignified as ever, "I've heard that bicycle riding is quite a healthy form of exercise."

Grandmary is quiet for a long time. I feel my heart thudding in my ears with each passing second.

Turn to page 126.

The next hour passes like days. Should I go home now? I finger my locket. Or can I make it till morning and say a proper good-bye to Samantha? I said good-bye to Stella only a few days ago—the thought of another good-bye makes me sad.

I lie down on my not-very-comfy bed of blankets, my stomach aching with hunger—and a sudden wave of homesickness. If I were at my dad's right now, I would have had dinner with my family, and then maybe taken a hot shower or bath. I'd call my mom or Stella, and then watch a movie before going to bed. But if I really were a wash girl, here in 1904, I couldn't do a single one of those things.

I curl into a ball, listening to the sounds of summer—children laughing and a dog barking—drifting through my window. Usually those sounds make me happy, but tonight I just feel lonely. I close my eyes and imagine that one of the voices I hear is my little stepsister's outside my bedroom door. I'm surprised by how much better that makes me feel.

Turn to page 125.

As we walk ashore, I breathe in the cool, pine-scented air. Samantha leads the way up the steep wooded path toward the house, which looks like a giant log cabin. I'm eager to see the inside, but suddenly Samantha veers left. "Grandmary, may we go straight to Wood Tick Inn?" she calls over her shoulder.

Wood Tick Inn? The sound of it makes my skin crawl, but when Samantha takes off down the path, what choice do I have but to follow her?

Along the way, Samantha shows me the other outbuildings. There's Rose Cottage, where Uncle Gard will sleep, and the boathouse, where the Admiral stays every summer.

"We're all so spread out!" I say, thinking of the crowded tent my family used to share when we went camping.

Samantha cocks her head. "It's funny," she says. "We all stay in different houses at Piney Point, but it's the only place where Grandmary, Uncle Gard, the Admiral, and I are ever all *together.* I love having all the people I care about most in one place. And now *you're* here, too."

Samantha gets a happy glint in her eye and says, "Race you to Wood Tick Inn!" She takes off down the path before me.

Turn to page 130.

The next morning, I don't leave my room until I'm fully dressed, my blankets are folded, and my hair is brushed. I didn't make a very good first impression with the people in Samantha's household. I'd like to do better today with whatever time I have left here.

Mrs. Hawkins is in the kitchen. She gives me her usual sympathetic expression and then offers me breakfast. I sit down and eat the most delicious blueberry muffin of my life. I wolf it down in seconds, and Mrs. Hawkins—with a wink—discreetly places another on my plate.

When Elsa enters the kitchen, she's oddly formal with me. "Come along, Ruby," she says. "Mrs. Edwards would like to see you now." The look on her face scares me. She's not angry with me. Instead she looks as if she, well, feels *sorry* for me. But why?

I follow Elsa into the parlor, my stomach flip-flopping. Mrs. Edwards is sitting in her high-backed chair with the same pitying expression on her face. My heart starts to pound.

Turn to page 127.

When Grandmary finally speaks, her tone has softened. "Samantha, that will be quite enough bicycle riding for one day."

"Yes, ma'am," Samantha says quickly. She looks relieved. She expected a worse scolding, I can tell. But then she surprises me by asking, "Grandmary, do you think I might do some more bicycling at Piney Point?"

I can't look at Grandmary, but when I glance at Samantha, I see that she's standing tall and looking straight into her grandmother's eyes. She really wants this. I cross my fingers behind my back.

Grandmary clears her throat. "Samantha," she says firmly. "There will be no more bicycling—"

My stomach clutches, anticipating Samantha's disappointment.

"—until we get you a safety bicycle, designed for young ladies. And until we make you some proper bloomers."

Grandmary is going to buy Samantha a bicycle. She's going to let her ride!

Turn to page 133.

Mrs. Edwards clears her throat. "Ruby, I've called a local orphanage to arrange for your return to the city. From there, the Children's Aid Society will place you on a train heading west with other orphans," she explains. "There are many fine families out west who will take in children to live with them."

"Grandmary, no!" It's Samantha, standing in the doorway. Her hands are balled into fists, and she's fighting back tears.

"Samantha, you know better than to eavesdrop," Mrs. Edwards scolds gently. "But now that you're here, please listen to me. The Children's Aid Society will help place Ruby in a good home. I truly believe that."

If she truly believes that, why does she look so sad for me?

Samantha must not believe her grandmother either. She runs from the parlor, and I fight the urge to race after my friend.

Mrs. Edwards's eyes are kind when she tells me that I will leave Mount Bedford on the train this morning. "Go upstairs now, Ruby," she says. "Elsa will draw you a hot bath."

I start to go upstairs, but first I want to check on

Samantha. She's in the kitchen, sitting beside Mrs. Hawkins, her face buried in the kind cook's shoulder. Hawkins, the butler, is there, too, polishing a silver teapot.

"Come sit, Ruby," Mrs. Hawkins says gently, nodding toward an empty chair.

Samantha lifts her tear-stained face and says, "Oh, Ruby, you *can't* go on that train. Where will you end up?"

"There, now," says Mrs. Hawkins, patting Samantha's arm. "That train might be young Ruby's best chance at finding a family of her own."

Samantha shakes her head. "We have to find a way to keep you here in Mount Bedford," she says stubbornly. "There *must* be a way."

Mrs. Hawkins sighs, but Hawkins clears his throat and says tentatively, "Perhaps there is a way. I heard from a good source in town that the Mount Bedford Glove Factory is looking for workers."

"That's it, Ruby!" Samantha says, jumping up. "You can earn your own money, and then *nobody* can send you away."

I'm not nearly as excited as Samantha is. Earn my

own money—at a factory? But I'm only ten years old!

Mrs. Hawkins looks doubtful, too. She turns to Hawkins and asks, "But where would she stay?"

"Ruby would be paid for her work," Hawkins says matter-of-factly. "And the factory runs a boarding house with rooms to rent for what I hear is a reasonable fee."

Everyone is looking at me, wondering what I'll say. An orphan train? Or working at a factory? If I take the train today, I can open my locket and be home by noon. But if I agree to factory work, I can spend more time with Samantha before she leaves for Piney Point tomorrow.

To agree to go to the factory tomorrow, turn to page 135.

To say good-bye to Samantha now, turn to page 132.

Pretty soon, we're settling into a tiny one-room cottage with windows overlooking the lake beyond. There are two beds in the room and a chair made out of tree branches. I take a quick look around. No sign of wood ticks. Phew!

I sit on my bed and bounce up and down a couple of times. Samantha says the beds are comfortable, but she *sometimes* sleeps on the porch of the cottage so that she can lie under the stars.

"Like camping?" I ask.

Samantha nods eagerly. And as it turns out, staying in Wood Tick Inn *does* feel like camping. After dinner, we wash up using cold water from an outdoor well and then talk by candlelight. Even though we've known each other for just a few days, we have so much to talk—and laugh—about! The last thing I remember before drifting off to sleep is the mournful sounds of the loons on the lake.

The next morning, I wake to a sharp knocking on the roof above my bed. I bolt upright.

Samantha giggles. "That's a woodpecker," she says,

"telling us it's time to get up!" She's already dressed in a navy blue dress and bonnet. Dressed for what?

"Should we go for a swim with Uncle Gard?" Samantha asks brightly. "I have another bathing dress you could wear."

A bathing dress? How could anyone swim with all those clothes on? I stare at the dress that covers her from knees to elbows. She also has on long stockings and shoes.

Samantha sees my expression and quickly says, "Or . . . we could pack a picnic and hike up the hill."

A hike sounds better than swimming wearing all those clothes, but I can tell Samantha is excited about swimming. Maybe I could sit on the shore and watch.

To agree to go swimming,
turn to page 149.

To watch Samantha swim,
turn to page 137.

To opt for hiking,
***go online to* beforever.com/endings**

I smile at Hawkins and then reach over to give Samantha a quick hug. "Thanks for wanting me to stay," I tell her, "but I think it's time for me to go meet my new family."

Samantha opens her mouth to protest, and then closes it again. She nods sadly.

Elsa bustles into the kitchen. "Ruby! Come along now. I've drawn a bath for you."

I give Samantha one last reassuring glance and then follow Elsa down the hall.

Upstairs, Elsa helps me take off the scratchy gray dress and step into the warm water. She takes the dress away to press it so that I will look "presentable" for the train. I think it's her way of being nice, now that she's not burdened with making a good servant out of me anymore. I want to tell Elsa that it's okay—that I know she tried her best with me. A city girl like me from the twenty-first century just isn't cut out for the work of a servant girl of long ago.

Turn to page 141.

The next morning, Samantha is still thanking me for teaching her how to ride. Her happiness is contagious. I can't help smiling, too, even though I'm going to be catching a train "home" in just a little while.

"I can't believe Grandmary is allowing me to ride a bicycle," says Samantha. "A bicycle!" She shakes her head and then says, "Grandmary surprises me every now and then. She's been my grandmother my whole life, but sometimes I feel as if I'm only just beginning to get to know her."

I wonder what that's like—living with someone you're only just getting to know. But wait, I *do* know what that's like. I picture my stepmom and little Gracie. If I try to get to know them—really try—will there be happy surprises in store for us, too? Suddenly I'm eager to go home and find out.

An hour later, I'm waving at Samantha and Hawkins through the window of the train as it pulls slowly away from the station. I close my eyes and try to capture an image of Samantha in my mind. She's riding a bike with her hair flowing freely behind her. She's wearing bloomers—her very own bloomers—and

she's smiling ear to ear, looking as if she's been riding her whole life. That's the image I keep with me as I snap open my locket.

Turn to page 147.

I'd like to try the factory," I say softly, wondering if I'm making the right decision. The relief on Samantha's face tells me that I am.

With Grandmary's permission, Hawkins calls the foreman at the glove factory, who says that I can report to work at 7:00 tomorrow morning.

But *today* promises to be all fun. Samantha seems determined to fill every minute with something special.

"Do you want to play Plum Pudding?" she asks.

Plum what? I giggle and then shrug. "Sure, sounds delicious."

As Samantha leads me out front and starts drawing a pattern on the walkway with a piece of chalk, I realize that "Plum Pudding" is just a fancy name for a game of hopscotch. I'm the first one to reach the "pudding" at the top of the pattern, but I'm pretty sure Samantha let me win.

After that, Hawkins sets up a net for us in the backyard and we play a game of tennis—or what he calls "lawn tennis." It's hard for me to get used to playing in the grass—and in a dress—but Samantha doesn't have any trouble at all. When I finally get a ball

over the net, she dives for it and sends it right back to me.

After two games of tennis, we plop down on the porch steps to catch our breath. "You're really good!" I say to Samantha.

"Thank you," she says, her cheeks flushed. "Uncle Gard taught me. I hope he'll play with me at Piney Point this week." Then she grows silent. Is she thinking about tomorrow, when we'll have to say good-bye?

"I think you're kind of lucky, Ruby," Samantha says suddenly.

"Lucky how?" I ask, wondering how Samantha can think that working at a factory is lucky.

"Well," says Samantha, "you'll make friends with *lots* of other girls at the boarding house—I know you will."

I'm not sure what to say to that. I tell Samantha that no matter how many new friends I meet, none will mean as much to me as she does.

Turn to page 144.

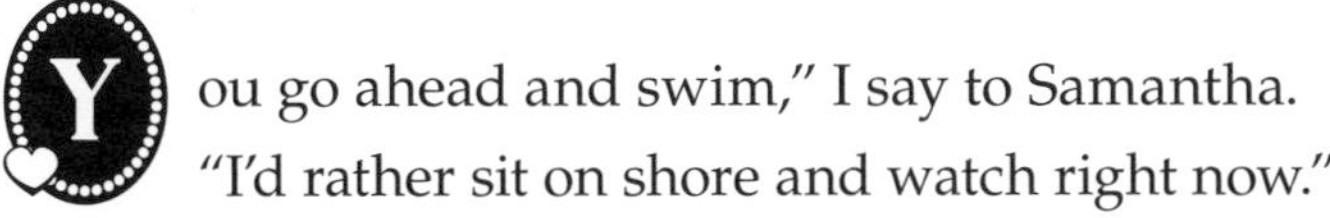

"You go ahead and swim," I say to Samantha. "I'd rather sit on shore and watch right now."

Samantha hesitates. "All right," she says. "But only for a little while. Then we'll do something fun together—I promise."

I get dressed quickly and follow Samantha down to the lake, where Uncle Gard is already swimming. He waves to us from the water. Cornelia is there, too, sitting on a blanket spread across the grass.

Samantha rushes into the cold water, squealing. She swims with long, confident strokes out to where Uncle Gard is treading water. She splashes him playfully and then swims past him, toward what looks like a large rock. A moment later, they're both pulling themselves up onto the rock.

That's when I hear Cornelia calling me over. "Come sit, dear," she says.

She pats a spot on the blanket, and I try to figure out the most ladylike way to sit in my dress. Crisscross applesauce doesn't seem like the best option. I see how Cornelia is leaning sideways, with her knees and feet drawn up beside her, and I try to mimic that pose without falling over.

Samantha waves to me from the rock and begins roughhousing with Uncle Gard. He stands up and pretends to wobble, as if falling backward. When he finally falls, he pulls Samantha with him into the water. They both come up laughing.

"She's having so much fun!" I say to Cornelia.

"Mmm-hmm," she says. She has lifted her face toward the sun, her eyes closed and a faint smile on her lips. "Piney Point makes us all feel a little more free, doesn't it?" she says. "I'd love to lose this itchy hat and soak up the sunshine. But my face would freckle in a matter of minutes."

I notice then that her skin is very fair, without a single freckle. And her ginger-colored hair seems almost red in the morning sun.

I glance back at Samantha and Uncle Gard. They have the same dark hair, wet and gleaming. "They look so much alike," I say.

"They certainly do," Cornelia says. "You should tell Samantha that. I think it would make her happy."

Samantha doesn't swim for long. She keeps glancing back at me, as if wondering whether I'm having a good time. Finally she hurries out of the water, drip-

ping wet, and tells me that she thinks she's had enough for the day.

As we walk back up the path toward Wood Tick Inn, I feel bad—as if I cut short her fun this morning. So I decide to tell her the truth.

"Samantha," I say, "I'm sorry I didn't swim with you. I'm just not used to swimming in so many clothes. I was kind of scared to try it."

Samantha turns to me, her eyes curious. She's shivering, her arms crossed at her chest. "Really?" she says. "What do you usually wear when you swim?"

I struggle with that question, picturing my two-piece bathing suit, but I finally say, "Well, for one thing, I don't wear shoes and stockings."

Samantha stops walking, her eyes wide. "Jiminy," she says under her breath. "Grandmary would never allow that, even here at Piney Point."

I remember then that Samantha doesn't get to choose what she wears. I suddenly feel ashamed, wondering what she must think of me and my choices. But I see the curiosity in her eyes when she asks, "Is the water cold on your legs? And do you mind feeling the lake bottom beneath your feet?"

I answer her questions as best I can. Then I tell her something else—how much I think she and Uncle Gard look alike—and Samantha's face lights up into the happiest of smiles. Cornelia was sure right about that.

Turn to page 155.

An hour later, after a sad good-bye with Samantha, I'm standing at the station with Elsa. Nerves rattle my stomach, as if I really *were* an orphaned girl about to hop a train in search of a family.

When a tall brunette woman in a black dress approaches, I instinctively shrink back. This must be the woman from the orphanage.

"Don't slouch, Ruby," Elsa scolds. She pulls me forward by the sleeve of my scratchy dress and introduces the woman as Mrs. Davis. Two young children are trailing Mrs. Davis, and they look as scared as I suddenly feel. The smaller of the two, a blond-haired boy, looks at me with wide eyes. I feel so sad for him that I have to look away.

Just then, someone taps my shoulder. I turn around and see . . . Samantha! She has brought a basket of warm gingerbread from Mrs. Hawkins. The smell alone makes my mouth water.

Then the train pulls into the station, and I have to say good-bye to Samantha all over again. She pulls me into a fierce hug.

"I'll be okay," I promise.

"I know you will, Ruby," Samantha says, but her

eyes are clouded with doubt. She gives me another hug.

Elsa almost hugs me, too, but seems to think better of it. She pats my arm awkwardly and hurries me up the steps of the train.

Turn to page 148.

It's late by the time Samantha and I go upstairs. There are two white nightgowns with pink ribbon trim laid out on the bed, and the corner of the bedspread is turned down, as if inviting us to climb inside. Did Elsa do that for us? How did she find the time between serving dinner and cleaning up?

Samantha offers me a spare toothbrush. I'm about to ask where the bathroom is when I see Samantha pour water from a pitcher into a bowl on her nightstand.

The wooden toothbrush Samantha hands me looks pretty normal, but instead of toothpaste, she pours black powder from a tin labeled "tooth powder" into a small bowl. I dip my wet toothbrush into the powder, which tastes salty and feels gritty against my teeth. But after I quickly brush and rinse a few times, I'm surprised to discover that my teeth feel smooth and clean.

As I inspect my teeth in the mirror, I scan my face and neck for red blisters, too. Ever since we left the doctor's office, I've felt itchy. No sign of any blisters yet. I breathe a sigh of relief.

Turn to page 152.

The next morning, as Hawkins and I take a bumpy ride across town in a horse-drawn cab, I discover a note, tied with a ribbon, in my apron pocket. It's from Samantha, who wishes me luck on my first day of work. She signs the letter, "Your friend always." I swallow the lump rising in my throat.

A few minutes later, I'm standing in the office of the heavyset, gray-haired foreman, who looks me over from head to toe. He starts listing off the many rules I'll need to follow here at the Mount Bedford Glove Factory. I try to focus, but I can barely hear him over the hum of the machines coming from the rooms beyond.

"You must be on time," he says. "Not a minute late, no excuses. No breaks until lunchtime. And your hair must be worn short."

That last rule gets my attention. "You mean, cut?" I ask timidly.

"Yes, cut short," he says, "so that it doesn't get caught in the winding machines. You can pull it back for today."

I nod, relieved, as I pull the ribbon from Samantha's note out of the pocket of my apron.

"Follow me to the knitting room," the foreman says. We hurry to a noisy room filled with about twenty workers—all young girls like me. Their eyes flicker nervously at the foreman, and then quickly back to their work. The foreman leads me toward a girl with cropped blonde hair sitting on a stool, winding yarn onto a cone. Her slender fingers are moving as quick as lightning.

"Mary," he says, "this girl will be your spare hand this week. See to it that she learns the job quickly, all right?"

Mary nods, but she doesn't seem happy about her new assignment.

When the foreman is gone, I introduce myself. "What grade are you in at school?" I ask brightly. "Do you know Samantha Parkington?"

Mary glances at the door, as if to make sure the foreman is gone, and then shakes her head. "I don't go to school," she says simply.

No school? How can girls as young as I am not go to school?

I have lots of questions for Mary, but she shuts me right down. "We're not allowed to talk while we work,"

she says quickly. “If we do, we won’t get paid.”

So much for making friends here at the factory. Suddenly, I miss Samantha.

Turn to page 150.

I am no longer moving forward. I'm sinking down, down, down . . . until I land, still sitting up, on the edge of a soft bed. I open my eyes and smile. I'm back in my capris and T-shirt, and a quick glance at the clock confirms that it's still, miraculously, 3:52.

From beyond the bedroom door, I hear voices—the voices of my family. As I jump up and open the door, I nearly trip over Gracie, who is standing there as if she's been waiting for me.

My stepmom looks up from her scrapbook in surprise. "Did you decide to join us?" she asks.

"Sort of," I say. "I was wondering if Gracie and I could play outside for a while. Would you like that, Gracie?"

My sister nods so hard that I'm afraid she's going to get dizzy. As we walk out of the house, hand in hand, I ask, "Gracie, do you know how to ride a two-wheel bike yet?"

She shakes her head no, which is *just* the answer I was hoping for.

The End

To read this story another way and see how different choices lead to a different ending, turn back to page 68.

After I've boarded the train, Mrs. Davis offers me a thin cardboard suitcase to hold my bundled clothing: my capris, T-shirt, and tennis shoes. The other two children with Mrs. Davis have the same kind of suitcase. What would that be like, trying to fit everything you owned into one small box?

I find an empty seat next to the little blond-haired boy. He turns away from me shyly, but then glances back, noticing my basket. He must smell the gingerbread.

I offer him a thick, warm piece. "Please," I urge him. "I can't eat it all by myself."

When the boy bites into the gingerbread, his face eases into a smile. Maybe it reminds him of a home he once knew—or of a home he dreams of having one day.

I reach for my locket, wondering how I'm going to get back to my own home now that I'm sitting next to this little boy. I fumble around my neck, feeling for my necklace. Where is it?

Then it hits me: I took off the necklace before I took my bath. *And I never put it back on!*

Turn to page 154.

Samantha loans me a bathing costume, which is like hers except it's black. I pull up the stockings and put on the slippers, too. Thinking about swimming in all these clothes makes my stomach knot up. Will they get waterlogged and heavy?

It'll be fine, I tell myself. *Samantha swims in these clothes all the time.* I muster up a smile and follow her out of the cabin. It's just a short walk down the path until we see sunshine sparkling off the lake.

Uncle Gard is already there. When he sees us, he plunges into the water and comes up shrieking and shivering, which makes Samantha giggle. Cornelia waves hello, too, from a blanket on the grass.

Samantha rushes into the water and swims behind Uncle Gard to a big rock about twenty yards from shore. She takes strong, sure strokes. I'm surprised by how well she swims, especially given that just a few strokes into the cool water, my clothes are wet and heavy. I feel as if I weigh three hundred pounds. By the time I can no longer touch bottom, I'm breathing hard.

Turn to page 159.

After watching Mary work for a while, I'm starting to sweat. It's really hot in the knitting room, and my legs and feet are getting sore from standing. "Can I go get a drink of water?" I ask Mary.

She shakes her head and says curtly, "No breaks until lunchtime." She must feel sorry for me, though, because she asks if I want to try winding the yarn. She passes it over to me, and, almost immediately, the yarn breaks. The winding machine grinds to a halt.

I glance up and see the other girls in the room looking at me—*glaring* at me. Mary quickly makes a knot to tie the yarn back together, and a tiny dark-haired girl who can't be more than six or seven starts up the machine again.

Mary doesn't offer me the yarn again, and I'm relieved. But it's getting hard to breathe in the stuffy room, and I hear a few of the girls coughing. There's a window on the far wall, but it's sealed shut.

When I think I can't stand the heat a second longer, I take a step away from the table and say to Mary, "I *really* need a break." She looks at me as if I just said I was going to fly to the moon.

"You can't!" she says, her brown eyes wide. "If you

stop working, you'll lose your pay!"

I don't care about my pay now. I just need some air. I hurry toward the door, but when I turn the knob, the door won't budge. *It's locked!* Why would the foreman lock us in here? To make sure we *don't* take breaks? Now I want to get out more than ever.

I start to panic, knocking loudly on the door, ignoring the horrified stares of the girls all around me. When the foreman finally opens the door, the thunderous look on his face makes my knees weak.

Turn to page 157.

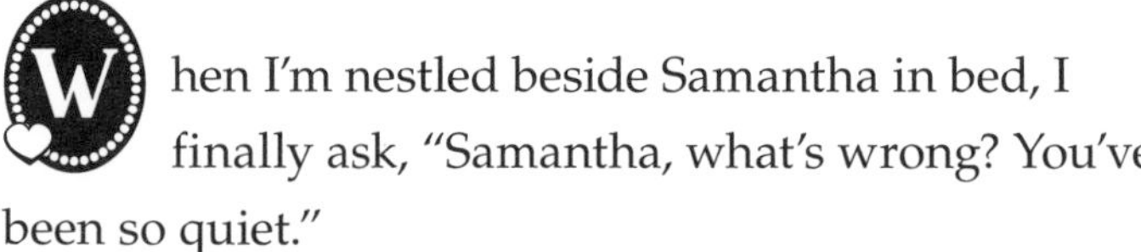

When I'm nestled beside Samantha in bed, I finally ask, "Samantha, what's wrong? You've been so quiet."

I can see her eyes, dark and brooding, in the glow of the wall lamp. She sighs. "I just don't understand Mrs. Ryland," she says. "Why shouldn't women be able to do interesting work like your mother does, or Dr. Ross? We should all try to help people whenever we can."

I don't know what to say, but Samantha doesn't seem to be looking for an answer. "I wish I could have a job like that one day," she says wistfully, "like your mother."

Samantha sounds a little sad, as if she's not sure her dream will come true. I wish I could tell her that things will change—that women will be able to vote, and there will be many more women doctors. But I wouldn't know how to explain how I know this. I can't very well tell her I'm from the future! Instead, I say, "Imagine having *Mrs. Ryland* as a mother."

Samantha turns to me, wide-eyed, and says, "Oh, I couldn't bear it!" Then she blurts out, "Worse yet, imagine having Eddie Ryland for a *brother*!"

We burst into giggles. We're still laughing when

Grandmary passes by our door and reminds us to settle down. Samantha reaches over to turn off the lamp beside her bed. As we cozy down again under the covers, she says to me, "I can imagine something much *better,* too."

"What?" I ask.

"Having you as a sister," she says softly.

My heart swells. Samantha *would* make a good sister. I think of the way she took care of me at the doctor's office.

And then I start worrying about chicken pox again. Will I come down with those horrible blisters like that girl at the doctor's office? Will I bring it home to my family, too? I suddenly picture my little stepsister's face covered with red blisters, and I squeeze my eyes shut, trying to wipe out the image. I open my eyes again and stare at the ceiling, wondering if sleep will ever come.

Turn to page 162.

I instantly realize what this means: No locket means no way home. No way home means I'm stuck on this train—this train that's about to leave the station.

I jump up and run toward the front of the train, but Mrs. Davis steps into the aisle to stop me. She forces me to sit back down in one of the front-row seats. I scan the windows for Elsa, but I know she's already gone.

Panicking, I wonder if the window's big enough for me to crawl through. That's when I see a face—a beautiful, familiar face. *Samantha.* She's still here, waving to me from the platform.

I force open the window before Mrs. Davis can stop me. "Samantha!" I call out.

Samantha rushes toward the window. "What is it?" she asks.

"My locket," I tell her quickly. "It's in the bathroom at your house, near the bathtub. I have to have it, Samantha. I *have* to!"

Samantha nods, determination washing over her face, and then she's running.

Turn to page 161.

After a day spent picking wildflowers and a delicious dinner at the main house, Samantha leads me back down the trail to Wood Tick Inn. The sun sinks low in the sky, casting red and orange hues over the lake.

As soon as we're inside our cabin, Samantha says, her eyes gleaming, "Let's go swimming."

My stomach drops. I'm still not sure I want to go into the water. "Yeah, but . . ." I stammer, trying to come up with an excuse, "isn't your bathing suit still wet?"

Samantha gives me a sly smile. "We're not wearing bathing suits," she says. "I've been thinking about what you wear when you swim. I think I might like to try it, too." She takes off her play dress and pinafore and peels off her stockings and shoes. Then she twirls in a circle wearing nothing but a lacy undershirt and long, lace-trimmed underpants.

"Really?" I say. "Are you sure?"

"I'm sure," says Samantha. "Now we can both swim. I want you to have fun here at Piney Point—as much fun as I have."

She looks so happy, as if she's ready for a great

adventure. So I quickly undress down to my undershirt and underpants, too, and we tiptoe to the lakeshore. Samantha holds a finger to her lips. "Be quiet," she whispers. "If Grandmary catches me out here in my underclothes, I can't even *imagine* what she'll say or do."

I watch Samantha's face as we step into the cool water. Her eyes are bright, and she shivers as she takes her first step. We both giggle, and she clamps her hand over her mouth. "Shh!" she reminds me.

We stay in shallow water—just up to our necks—and bounce on our toes. It's dusk now, and the moon shines bright overhead. "I feel so free in the water," Samantha confesses to me. "It's wonderful!"

I'm about to respond when we hear a woman's voice calling from the trail above. "Samantha!"

Turn to page 165.

The foreman leans forward, his angry face an inch from mine, and demands to know what I want. I can't speak. He orders me back into the room with a scowl and a pointed finger. The door slams shut, and I hear the click of the lock.

My heart throbs in my chest as I try to think. It's time for me to go—I know that now. But I have to get a message to Samantha first.

I fumble in my pocket for the note she left me this morning, and then I rush toward Mary's table, searching for something to write with. I find a pencil stub resting by a measuring tape. I feel Mary's eyes on me as I scrawl a message on the back of Samantha's note. It reads:

Dear Samantha,

The factory job didn't work out. I had to leave Mount Bedford—there's a home waiting for me out there. But I hope to see you again one day.

Your friend always,

Ruby

I fold the letter and write "Samantha Parkington"

on the front. Then I glance toward the door, making sure the foreman is truly gone. I don't want to get Mary into trouble, but I need her help.

"Mary," I say, "will you please find a way to get this letter to my friend Samantha Parkington? It's very, *very* important."

Mary furrows her brow. Her eyes keep flickering toward the door. *Please, please help me,* I plead silently, and finally Mary nods.

"Thank you," I say, setting the letter down beside her. I don't know if the letter will make it to Samantha, but I do know that I have to leave this room.

Turn to page 163.

I keep swimming, stroke after stroke, each more difficult than the last. I put my face in the water and kick, but my legs sink downward, and in this wet, bunched-up outfit, I can't reach forward with my arms. I feel as if I'm swimming in place.

When I look up and see that Samantha and the rock are still really far away, I start to panic, taking shorter, quicker strokes. The weight of the water pulls me downward, and I can't catch my breath. My head bobs under the water once, and I lunge back up, gasping for air and looking wildly around me for something to grab on to.

I hear someone—Cornelia, maybe—calling Gard's name, and then I sink under the water again. I grab at the water as if it were slow-drying cement. When I come up the second time, I see a dark head swimming toward me with lightning-quick strokes. *Uncle Gard.*

I go under one more time saying his name, taking in a mouthful of water, but he's got me now. He hooks his arm under my chin and tows me back to shore. Cornelia meets us there and helps us out of the water. I can't stop coughing.

I finally catch my breath and then look up to see

Samantha swimming quickly toward shore. When she reaches me, she's wild-eyed with concern. "Are you all right?" she asks.

At first I can't talk at all—I'm afraid I'll start crying. My heart is pounding so loud that I'm sure everyone around me can hear it.

Samantha apologizes to me over and over again, and when I can finally speak, I try to tell her that it's not her fault—I just made a bad decision. I don't tell her that I was swimming with *way* more clothes than I'm used to.

As we're walking back to Wood Tick Inn with Uncle Gard on one side of me and Cornelia on the other, Samantha glances over her shoulder at me with every step. And even after breakfast, as we're sitting on the porch steps of the main house, she looks so sad. I feel as if I've already ruined our first day together at Piney Point. I need to try to make it better.

Turn to page 169.

I try to picture Samantha's path to her home. It's not far, just down the street. It took Elsa and me ten minutes to walk here. How long will it take Samantha to run? Will she make it back before the train leaves?

If she doesn't, I'll go forward into the future with only the few possessions in the cardboard suitcase at my feet. No laptop, no cell phone, no way to call home. No photos of my family. No *family* at all.

My heart pounds in my ears, and I count the beats like seconds: *one, two, three . . . ninety-two, ninety-three . . . two hundred and one, two hundred and two . . . Samantha, please hurry!*

When the train whistle blows, I jump out of my seat. Suddenly, I can't catch my breath. I stare out the window, willing Samantha to appear. *Please, please, please!*

Turn to page 168.

Sleep does come, but in the middle of the night I wake up with a start. The room is dark, and I'm not sure where I am. When I remember what happened at the doctor's office, I'm anxious to check my face in the mirror for chicken pox.

In the moonlight shining through the window, I see Samantha sleeping beside me. I don't want to wake her. I touch my face, searching for bumps or blisters. I don't feel anything. I lie back in relief.

Part of me wants to stay and get to know Samantha better. The other part of me, though, is "itching" to go home. I need to call my mom to ask if I've ever had the chicken pox.

I could leave a note for Samantha and go home right now, but I know how sad she'd be to wake up and find me gone. What do I do? The longer I lie still, the more anxious and itchy I feel.

To leave right now, turn to page 166.

To wait until morning, turn to page 178.

I want to open my locket and just disappear, but I can't do that in front of Mary. So instead, I take a breath of courage and step toward the locked door. I raise my fist and pound as loudly as I can.

It's only seconds before the foreman answers, and when he sees me again, he looks as if he's about to explode with rage. Before he can speak, I holler the words "I quit!" Ducking beneath his arm, I race down the hall toward an open door.

As soon as I feel the rush of cool outside air, I reach for my locket and snap it open. I'm dizzy for a moment, and then I'm back in my room—my air-conditioned room—with soft carpet beneath my tired feet. In the silence of the room, I realize that my ears are ringing. The *clack* and *whir* of the winding machines is gone, but my ears don't know it yet.

I'm wearing my capris and T-shirt again. The scratchy dress is gone. As I sink down onto my bed, I say a private thank-you to the universe that I'm not an orphan in Samantha's time. I can go home, to a world where I don't have to work, where I have parents who love me, where I can get an ice-cold glass of water whenever I need one. I can barely open my bedroom

door and get to the kitchen faucet fast enough. But as I leave my room, I touch my locket and say thank you to Samantha, too, who taught me a lot about trying to help others—and appreciating all I have right now.

The End

To read this story another way and see how different choices lead to a different ending, turn back to page 129.

Samantha's jaw drops. "Hurry!" she whispers as she starts swimming around the pier. She takes graceful, noiseless strokes. I try to do the same, but there's nothing graceful about my breaststroke.

When we reach the shore, we crawl out of the water and duck down behind the pier. Samantha looks terrified. That's when I realize what a risk she took for me. What will happen if Grandmary finds her out here, swimming in her underwear?

I peek my head above the pier for just an instant and see the shadowy figure of a woman standing on shore. But it's not Grandmary. It's Cornelia.

"Samantha?" she calls again. She sounds worried.

"What do we do?" I whisper to Samantha.

Samantha steels herself and stands up. "I'm here, Miss Cornelia," she says, her voice shaky. She doesn't meet Cornelia's eyes, but instead looks down at her own bare legs and feet, shamefaced.

Turn to page 173.

I start easing myself out of bed, one leg at a time. The floor creaks, and I freeze, listening for any change in Samantha's breath. It takes what seems like hours to tiptoe across the floor and get dressed, but it's worth it. After a long evening spent wearing skirts, my T-shirt and capris feel light and free. They feel like home.

I find notepaper on Samantha's desk and write a good-bye note. It says:

Dear Samantha,

I woke up and remembered where I was heading before I met you. My family's waiting for me—I have to catch the first train out of Mount Bedford.

Thank you for being a good friend and for taking such great care of me while I was here. I'll never forget you.

I try to think of something else to say, and then it comes to me. I write:

Samantha, keep your eyes on the future—on your dreams. And remember: things are changing all the time.

I put the note on Samantha's nightstand and sneak out into the hallway. As I reach for the locket around my neck, I feel a pang of guilt for leaving this way. Samantha was so good to me at the doctor's office. She was brave when I couldn't be. *I wish I had her courage,* I think as I snap open the locket.

Turn to page 171.

There she is! Samantha is racing along the platform toward me, something shiny dangling from her hand. My locket!

I lean through the open window, my own hand outstretched. When Samantha reaches me, she forces the necklace into my hand, pressing her palm against mine to be sure she doesn't drop the locket. I grip it with my fingers and hold Samantha's hand close, too.

She's out of breath, and I'm still having trouble catching mine, so we say nothing. But we lock eyes, and I squeeze her hand until the train starts slowly moving forward. When Samantha is a few yards away, I finally get the words out: *"Thank you."*

Samantha nods and waves until I can't see her anymore. Then I turn around in my seat and clutch the necklace to my chest. Just before I open the locket, I take one last look behind me at the little blond-haired boy. *I'm going home,* I think to myself, *but that little boy can't.* I swallow an overwhelming wave of sadness, sink down in my seat, and pry the locket open.

Turn to page 177.

amantha," I say, scooting closer to her on the porch steps, "I'm sorry I scared you."

When Samantha looks up, I'm surprised to see tears in her eyes. "It's not your fault," she says. "The lake . . . it's . . ." She bites her lip, as if she doesn't want to say another word. Big tears start rolling down her face.

It takes a long time for Samantha to tell me what's wrong, but she finally says, her voice quivering, "My parents drowned in that lake. Their boat got caught in a storm. When I saw you go under the water, I was afraid that . . . that I would lose you, too."

Samantha's words hit me like a blow to the ribs. *Now* I understand why she was so scared when she saw me struggling in the water.

I try to think of what to say or do. I remember how nice Samantha was when I told her that I missed my mother. I want to be a good listener, too, so I ask, "What were your parents like, Samantha? Does Grandmary tell you stories about them?"

She wipes her eyes and shakes her head. "Grandmary doesn't talk about my parents," she says. "I think it makes her miss them too much."

"But it helps to talk about the good memories, doesn't it?" I ask. It's something my mom says whenever I miss my dad.

Samantha nods. "I think so, too," she says. She smiles, but there's a faraway look in her eyes. I wish there was more I could do for her.

Turn to page 175.

I brace myself for the impact, but when it comes, it's soft and welcoming. I open my eyes and find myself back in the room I share with Gracie, dressed in my capris and T-shirt. It seems as if days have passed, but the clock still says 3:52. And there, beside the clock, is my cell phone.

I call my mother immediately, using the work number that she programmed into my phone. When I hear her voice, my heart leaps. I miss her so much!

Mom sounds worried. "What is it, honey?" she asks. "Is something wrong?"

"No, Mom," I say. At least I hope not. "I'm just wondering, have I ever had the chicken pox?" I hold my breath, waiting for her response.

When she says no, my stomach drops. But then she adds, "You were vaccinated against it when you were little. You don't need to worry."

Vaccinated? A cool wave of relief washes away the fear—and itchiness—I've been feeling. I'm safe.

I think of the shots I've gotten over the years, the ones I dreaded but never thought much about afterward. Then I think of that little girl and her brother who were covered in blisters from head to toe. Will

there be vaccinations for children in Samantha's time?

Someday, I tell myself. And there'll be more women doctors giving those vaccinations, too. Will Samantha be one of them? One thing's for sure: I know she'll find a way to help other people, just as she helped me today.

The End

To read this story another way and see how different choices lead to a different ending, turn back to page 15.

We both stand, shivering in the cool evening air, waiting for the scolding. But instead Cornelia says, "Goodness! A moonlight swim. How delightful."

Samantha looks up, surprised. "Are you going to tell Grandmary?" she asks.

Cornelia pauses. "I do think your grandmother would be concerned about your safety," she says. "Don't you? It's always wise to have an adult swim with you."

Samantha hesitates. "But . . . are you going to tell her what we're wearing?" she asks in a small voice.

Cornelia glances at our "swimsuits," and a hint of a smile passes her lips. "Those aren't the most proper of bathing dresses," she says, "but I must say, they're quite practical. I've never understood why women have to wear long sleeves and stockings in the water. They are just more layers to dry off when you're done."

Samantha's shoulders relax, and she smiles when Cornelia says, "In fact, you girls have inspired me. Would you mind if I joined you?"

As Cornelia unlaces her boots and pulls off her stockings, one by one, Samantha giggles and casts me an I-can't-believe-this-is-happening glance. And when

Cornelia pulls up her skirts and wades into the water, Samantha rushes in right beside her. I hang back on shore for a moment, watching them laugh and splash together in the cool lake water. They both look so free and happy.

Samantha took a risk to make sure that I felt safe and could have fun in the water. But watching her now, I wonder if maybe I helped *her* a little bit, too. I brace myself for the cool water and race into the lake after my friend.

The End

To read this story another way and see how different choices lead to a different ending, turn back to page 131.

The next morning, Samantha and I wake to raindrops. We hurry to the main house, where the others are settled in the living room. A fire burns in the big stone fireplace, and the Admiral sits in the rocking chair to one side, napping with an open book on his chest. Grandmary sits doing needlework in the rocker on the other side of the fireplace.

Delicious smells waft in from the kitchen, where Mrs. Hawkins is hard at work. *This is sure no vacation for her,* I think to myself as I sink down onto the couch beside Samantha and Cornelia.

Lying on the bearskin rug in front of the fireplace, Uncle Gard tells Grandmary about a play he and Cornelia saw in the city. He starts acting out a scene in the play, and then pauses and asks, "Hey, Sam, how about a game of charades? Who am I?" He jumps up and pretends that his hands are bound behind his back.

Samantha giggles and shouts, "Harry Houdini!"

Then Samantha pretends to ride horseback while shooting a rifle at an imaginary target. Grandmary guesses Annie Oakley, which means she's up next.

Grandmary thinks for a minute and then sets down

her needlework. She lifts an imaginary paintbrush and begins dabbing at an invisible canvas. After a few wrong guesses, Samantha says, "Mary Cassatt!"

I know who Houdini and Annie Oakley were, but I've never heard of Mary Cassatt. When I ask Samantha who she is, Samantha steps toward the bookshelf to show me a book of paintings. That's when I see a small oval picture frame. The teenage girl in the photo could be Samantha—her hair dark and eyes pretty.

"Samantha?" I ask hesitantly. "Is this your mother?"

Samantha's cheeks flush and she nods. "Her name was Lydia," she says quietly.

Turn to page 182.

I'm falling downward, gripping the locket. I land on my bed and open my eyes to see that I'm dressed in my capris and T-shirt. I bury my face in my pillow and let the tears come.

Someone knocks on my door and asks if she can come in. It's Gracie. She doesn't wait for an answer, and I'm glad, because I don't think I could speak right now.

When Gracie sees me crying, she pats me on the back as if she were the big sister, not me. That makes me cry harder, but I'm afraid I'll scare Gracie, so I try to pull it together.

"Are you sad?" she asks, looking up at me.

I shake my head. "I was before," I say. "I was kind of homesick. But I feel much better now."

Gracie smiles. "Do you want to play with me?" she asks. This time, I say yes. It feels like days since I've seen her, and I realize—with horror—that if Samantha had been a minute late, it might have been a lifetime. I hang on to Gracie's hand and let her lead me out of the room.

The End

To read this story another way and see how different choices lead to a different ending, turn back to page 129.

I want to go home right now, but Samantha has been so good to me that I need to say good-bye to her face to face. So I force myself to lie still, thinking of how calm *she* was with me at the doctor's office. I try to be that way for her now.

When dawn light finally trickles through the window, I'm staring at the ceiling, trying to remember my mom's phone number at work. Samantha's voice breaks the silence. "What are you thinking?" she asks.

"I remember where I was heading yesterday, Samantha," I tell her. I've been waiting for what seems like a hundred hours to have this conversation, so the words spill right out. "I'm supposed to be staying with relatives in a town a few hours north of here," I explain.

Samantha sits up and says, "That's wonderful! You remember!" She's happy for me—of course she is—but I see the moment when she realizes what this means for her. The smile leaves her eyes and she says, "You'll be leaving soon then, won't you?"

I nod. "I should catch a train north first thing this morning," I say.

Samantha nods and says, "I understand. Your relatives must be really worried about you. I'll tell

Grandmary." She starts to climb out of bed.

"Samantha, wait," I say.

She hesitates and her face brightens, as if she hopes I've changed my mind.

"I just want to say that you really helped me yesterday," I say. "You made me feel welcome here and less scared at the doctor's office. I know you're going to find a way to help people one day, just like Dr. Ross does—and my mother."

Samantha blushes. She's smiling when she says, "I hope you're right." As she leaves the room, she's nearly skipping.

After she's gone, I think about what I'll do when I get back home. The first thing I'll do is call my mother. I want to ask her if I've ever had the chicken pox, but there's something I want to say even more—that I'm proud of her, and the work she does. That I feel lucky to be her daughter. And that one day, I hope I grow up to be someone who helps people, just like her.

The End

To read this story another way and see how different choices lead to a different ending, turn back to page 15.

Samantha and I look at each other in horror.

"Elsa said she's leaving on the next train out of Mount Bedford," says Samantha. "We have to get to the station and catch her before she leaves!"

"Wait. Should we tell Grandmary?" I ask.

Samantha glances toward the house and shakes her head. "There's no time," she says. "Let's go!"

We race toward the station, which Samantha says is just down the street. Even so, we're huffing and puffing by the time we get there. I'm relieved to see Elsa sitting on a bench. She looks up, clearly surprised to see us.

After Samantha explains what happened, Elsa sniffs. "No matter," she says in a cool tone. "It was time for me to go home anyway. My mother's been ill for months. I've been saving money to help her pay her doctor bills."

Doctor bills. Is that why Elsa had a stack of bills in her closet? I wonder how long it took her to save that money if she's earning what I'm earning: just a dollar a week. The thought makes me feel sick to my stomach.

Turn to page 184.

The next day, it's time for me to go home, or as Samantha puts it, "to go visit my family." Hawkins helps me board the steamboat. My last image of Samantha is of her waving to me from the dock, her golden brooch sparkling in the sunlight. Grandmary is there, too, her arm around Samantha.

I play with my own locket. Which photos would I put in it if I could open it and have time stand still? My mom's, of course. And my dad's. But then I think of my stepmother and remember her words: "This locket helped me through a pretty tough time." Something flutters in my chest—the realization that maybe my *stepmom* had some adventures with this locket, too. Did she travel back in time and meet Samantha?

When I get home, maybe I'll ask my stepmom about the "tough time" she went through when she was my age. She may not want to talk about it. Or, then again, maybe she will. It's good to talk about these things. I know that for certain now, and I hope that Samantha, my new friend, does, too.

The End

To read this story another way and see how different choices lead to a different ending, turn back to page 131.

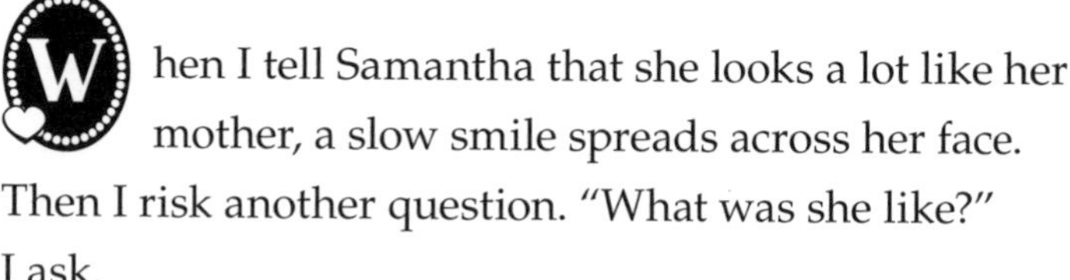

When I tell Samantha that she looks a lot like her mother, a slow smile spreads across her face. Then I risk another question. "What was she like?" I ask.

I know Samantha doesn't remember her mother, so I'm really asking Grandmary. I risk a glance in her direction. Her needle is poised in the air, and her mouth is pursed. I wait, hoping that she will talk to us. *Please, please, please . . .*

Grandmary sets down her needlework. "Your mother, Samantha, was curious, happy, and generous," Grandmary begins slowly. "She was an artist who loved sketching and painting with watercolors, and she especially loved long summer days here at Piney Point, just as you do."

When Grandmary adds, "Your mother was very much like *you*, Samantha," I see tears in Samantha's eyes. Grandmary sees them, too. As she crosses the room to come sit beside Samantha, I excuse myself, saying I'll go see what Mrs. Hawkins has cooking in the kitchen.

A short while later, Samantha finds me there and gives me a warm hug. She shows me something that

Grandmary gave her: a golden brooch locket. When Samantha flips it open, I see two people: Lydia, all grown up, and a handsome dark-haired man with a neat beard. "My father," Samantha says, smiling. "Grandmary wants me to wear it, to remember my parents—always."

I finger my own locket, dangling from my neck. Samantha asks, "Do you have pictures of your family in your locket?"

I shake my head. "No," I say, and then add, "not yet."

Turn to page 181.

I'm sorry your mother's ill," Samantha says. "Will you come back to the house before you go, Elsa? I know Grandmary will want to speak with you, especially after I tell her what happened."

Elsa looks at Samantha, doubt in her eyes. That's when Samantha adds in a very sincere voice, "I'm sorry I accused you of stealing, Elsa. I really am."

Elsa nods ever so slightly. Then she does something completely unexpected. She turns and apologizes to *me*.

"I'm sorry I accused you, too, Ruby," she says. "There was no cause for that."

I blush and instantly feel guilty. I was so mad about being accused of stealing, yet I turned around and treated Elsa the same way. Next time, I won't judge someone so quickly—not without giving her a chance.

I wonder when that "next time" will be. I think of my stepmom and stepsister, whom I haven't really tried to get to know. They deserve a chance, too, I realize, as Samantha and I lead Elsa down the platform steps toward home.

The End

To read this story another way and see how different choices lead to a different ending, turn back to page 33.

ABOUT Samantha's Time

When Samantha was growing up, the whole world seemed to be changing. If she listened closely, she could hear the sounds of new inventions: telephones ringing, electric lights buzzing, and automobiles rumbling. In factories, machines produced goods more swiftly and cheaply than human hands ever could. In 1904, the brand-new century was called "the Age of Confidence" because many Americans were certain that progress would improve their lives.

Not everyone was so certain. Some people, like Grandmary, believed they got along just fine before machines and people filled their lives with noise and new ideas. They didn't see the need to change the old ways.

But things did change—especially for girls and women. They began playing sports that were previously only considered proper pastimes for men. By the turn of the century, ladies were bicycling, practicing gymnastics, and playing lawn tennis. With these new sports came new ideas about fashion. Until then, girls and women wore only skirts and dresses. Then fitness-minded ladies began wearing *bloomers*, or full pants gathered at the knee. Many people did not think pants were appropriate clothing for women, but "bloomer girls" soon became a common sight.

People's growing interest in exercise as a road to good health triggered all kinds of new health-care products. New medicines, such as aspirin, and the discovery that germs spread disease made Samantha's world a safer and healthier place to live. Women were studying medicine, and by 1904, hundreds of "lady doctors" were at work across the country.

Many women went into the new field of social work. Known as *reformers,* these women worked to improve the quality of life for everyone, but especially for poor people and immigrants. Many reformers wanted to make sure factories and other workplaces were safe.

Social workers also helped children who were orphaned. Thousands of orphans from New York City were sent west on trains with the hope of being adopted. Farming families who needed extra workers for the fields often took in orphans. Sometimes they adopted a brother but not his sister. Those orphans who didn't find a new home returned on the train to New York City.

When Samantha was a young girl, women could not vote in elections. People who believed that women should vote were called *suffragists.* Like Samantha's Aunt Cornelia, they fought hard to convince America that they were right. They marched through city streets carrying signs, gave speeches, and went door-to-door asking people to sign petitions. Finally, in 1920, when Samantha would have been 25 years old, a law was passed giving women the right to vote. Samantha might have driven to the polling booth in her own Model T automobile!

Read more of SAMANTHA'S stories,

available from booksellers and at *americangirl.com*

Classics

Samantha's classic series, now in two volumes:

Volume 1:
Manners and Mischief
Making friends with a servant isn't proper for a young lady—but that won't stop Samantha!

Volume 2:
Lost and Found
Samantha finally finds her friend Nellie—living in an orphanage! She's determined to help Nellie escape.

Journey in Time

Travel back in time—and spend a day with Samantha!

The Lilac Tunnel
What is it really like to live in Samantha's world? What if you're a servant rather than a proper young lady? Find out by choosing your own path through this multiple-ending story.

Mysteries

More thrilling adventures with Samantha!

Clue in the Castle Tower
Samantha's visiting a grand English manor—haunted by a ghost!

The Cry of the Loon
A series of strange accidents at Piney Point has Samantha worried.

The Curse of Ravenscourt
Samantha has a new home—and it's putting everyone in danger!

The Stolen Sapphire
Samantha realizes that someone on her steamship is a jewel thief.

A Sneak Peek at

Manners and Mischief

A Samantha Classic

Volume 1

What happens to Samantha?
Find out in the first volume of her classic stories.

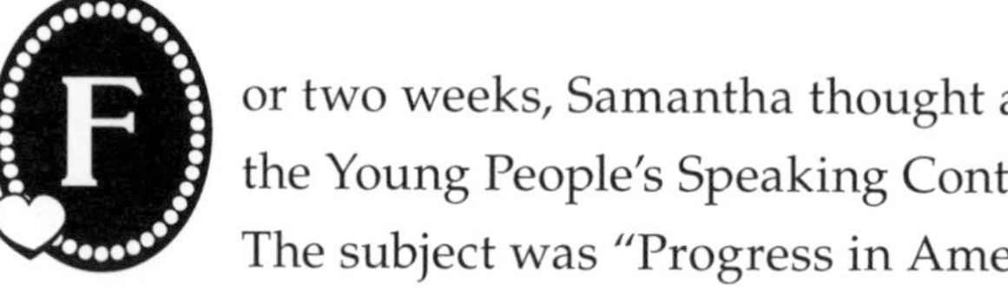

For two weeks, Samantha thought about the Young People's Speaking Contest. The subject was "Progress in America." She read books about new inventions. She took notes about the ideas she got from talking to different people. Mrs. Hawkins said the best invention was the gas stove because it didn't get full of ashes like a coal stove, and you didn't have to keep coals hot all night and all summer. She said that was progress. And Hawkins told Samantha about factories. He said factories were the most important sign of progress in America because there was no end to what they could make. He said they made things fast and they made things cheap. And he said that meant there were more things for more people all over the country. That started Samantha thinking about the speech she would write.

After lunch on Thursday, all the girls in Miss Crampton's Academy filed quietly into the assembly room. They stood in front of their chairs until they had sung a hymn and said a prayer. Then they sat down

with their backs straight and their hands folded in their laps. There was no whispering even before Miss Crampton began speaking.

"As you know, two girls from this Academy will represent all of us at the Speaking Contest tomorrow evening," Miss Crampton said. "Today, Miss Stevens and I will choose those two girls. They will be the two girls who give the best speeches about progress in America."

Even with her hands folded, Samantha managed to cross her fingers. She took deep breaths to steady herself.

At last Samantha's turn came. She was the last girl to speak. Her voice was clear and steady.

"American factories are the finest in the world," she began. "They are true signs of our progress. It used to take many hours to make a pair of shoes or a table by hand. Now machines can make hundreds of shoes and hundreds of tables in just a few hours. And they make thread and cloth, toys and bicycles, furniture, and even automobiles. These things cost less money than they used to because they are made by machines. So now more people can buy the things they want and the

things they need. That is progress. Truly, we could not go forward into the twentieth century without our factories and without our machines. They are the greatest sign of progress in America."

There was applause in the room. Miss Stevens nodded in approval. Samantha beamed as she walked back to her seat.

Miss Crampton looked immensely pleased as she stepped to the front of the room. "All of our young ladies have done a splendid job," she said. "I am proud of each one of them. And now, it gives me great pleasure to announce our winners. Will Miss Samantha Parkington please step forward?"

Samantha rose and walked to the front of the room again. Miss Crampton handed her an award. She felt her heart swell with pleasure as she heard the applause around her.

In Mount Better School that afternoon, Nellie watched proudly as Samantha pinned her award to the wall. "Can I hear your speech, Samantha?" Nellie

asked. There was no doubt in Nellie's mind that her friend's speech would be the best ever written since Abraham Lincoln's.

Samantha repeated her speech just as she had at the Academy, remembering with a thrill the applause that had followed it. She finished proudly and then looked at Nellie for the praise she was sure would be coming.

But Nellie was staring at the floor and running her finger along the edge of the cushion.

"Well?" asked Samantha.

"It's very nice," said Nellie in a voice that said she didn't think it was nice at all.

Samantha felt hurt. "What's the matter with it?" she asked.

"It's very nice. It's just . . . well, it's just not very true," said Nellie.

"What do you mean?"

"I used to work in a factory, Samantha. It's not like that."

Nellie *had* worked in a factory. Samantha had almost forgotten that. "Well, what's a factory like, then?" she asked.

Nellie was quiet. She was remembering things

she didn't want to remember. "I worked in a big room with other kids," she said finally. "Twenty others, I guess. But that didn't make it fun. We couldn't play. We couldn't even talk. The machines were too noisy. They were so noisy that when I got home at night my ears were buzzing, and it was a long time before I could hear anything. We had to go to work at seven in the morning, and we worked until seven at night. Every day but Sunday."

Nellie continued, "I worked on the machines that wound the thread. There were hundreds of spools. We had to put in new ones when the old ones got full, and we tied the thread if it broke. We had to stand up all the time. I got so tired, Samantha. My back hurt and my legs hurt and my arms got heavy. The machines got fuzz and dust all over everything. It was in the air, and it got in my mouth and made it hard to breathe."

Nellie was quiet again. Then she went on. "The room was awful hot in summer. But it was worse in winter because there wasn't any heat. Our feet nearly froze. We couldn't wear shoes."

Samantha was shocked. "You couldn't wear shoes?" she asked.

"We had to climb on the machines to change the spools, and shoes could make us slip. The machines were so strong, they could break your hand or your foot or pull a finger off as easy as anything. We all had to have our hair short. If your hair was long, the machines could catch it and pull it right out. They just kept winding. Once I saw that happen to a girl. She was just standing there, and then suddenly she was screaming and half her head was bleeding. She almost died."

Nellie was running her finger along the edge of the cushion again. "They paid us one dollar and eighty cents a week." She looked straight at her friend. "That's why thread is so cheap."

Samantha stared at Nellie. She couldn't move. She felt numb and cold, but her scalp was tingling and her arms had a strange ache in them.

About the Author

As a girl growing up in southern Wisconsin, ERIN FALLIGANT loved exploring her great-grandmother's house, which was built in the early 1900s. As she tiptoed up and down the servants' staircase, she imagined what it must have been like to grow up at that time in such a grand home. Like Samantha, Erin could often be found high in the branches of the trees in her backyard. She spent her summer days writing stories—and dreaming of becoming an author. Some dreams come true! Erin has written many American Girl advice, activity, and fiction books. She enjoys writing multiple-ending books because it's fun to imagine the many paths each story could take. In her free time, Erin coaches Girls on the Run, helping girls build self-confidence and run paths of their own near her home in Madison, Wisconsin.